Praise for *Show Them a Good Time*

"At its best, which is often, Flattery's prose has a thrilling relentlessness and rhythmical snap to it; it pummels and excites." —*The Guardian*

"Flattery puts across finely observed everyday details with an absurd sensibility and has a talent for one-liners." —*The New Yorker*

"Just when we think we know where Flattery is going, she disorients us by changing tack and veering off-course into surreal territory . . . The best tales blend personal pain and mordant wit, and are seductively offbeat and pleasingly on point." —*Star Tribune* (**Minneapolis–St. Paul**)

"Flattery is a rising star . . . Her debut collection is a magnificently mordant work, full of delicious one-liners, perennially creeping menace, and hypnotically nihilistic depictions of cold-eyed young women trapped in strange, lonely, sometimes dystopian situations . . . Reminiscent of the writing of Mary Gaitskill, Lorrie Moore, and Ottessa Moshfegh, *Show Them a Good Time* is a deft and dazzling work of pitch-black humor and deep, disquieting sorrow." —**LitHub**

"Fabulously entertaining . . . very funny stuff. The pages just glide by, but there's really difficult material and really knotty emotions thrumming along just beneath the blithe surface of things." —**Kevin Barry, The Millions**

"Brilliant . . . Ten smart stories about dating, relationships and the absurdities of modern life." —**Elle.com**

"Highly addictive . . . Flattery's off-kilter voice blends chatty candour and hard-to-interpret allegory (think Diane Williams or Lorrie Moore), with the deadpan drollery and casually disturbing revelations heightened by her fondness for cutting any obvious connective tissue between sentences." —*The Observer*

"Mind-blowing; by turns macabre, ferociously funny and concerned with what's been called 'the dark comedy of women's lives.' Like Rooney, Flattery sometimes focuses on the idea of 'normal' as a surreal concept with one character describing her hometown in Ireland as 'a strange place dressed up as a normal place.'" —*The Globe and Mail*

"Flattery's judgments crackle with cruel, clear sight . . . The book's epigraph comes from Lorrie Moore, who is an obvious influence on the high-wire style, those seductive insights armored with glittering wit against the pain they describe. Flattery writes with empathy, freedom and virtuosic technique: this debut announces the arrival of a brilliant talent." —*Financial Times*

"The book is a bit like drinking: refreshingly obliterative, realistically distorted . . . some of the most concrete aspects of the book are provided by the dialogue, which, as in Lorrie Moore or Deborah Eisenberg, often contains much of the stories' movement as it delivers funny little zaps to the main character's perspective." —*London Review of Books*

"Nicole Flattery's short stories stab and slip, cutting without immediately alerting you to that fact . . . What sticks is her deadpan stare, the precision of her humor— that feeling that sometimes the funniest person in the room is the one who isn't laughing." —**The A.V. Club**

"Flattery, whose stories have been compared to Lorrie Moore's, depicts dead-end jobs and the grinding fear of poverty. While her style is jaunty and enlivening— Groucho Marx funny—her young women are even less hopeful than Moore's. They're held hostage by the economic machinery of their lives . . . Beneath the one-liners and clever dark comedy, *Show Them a Good Time* shows real daring." —*Bookforum*

"A seamless blend of reality and the surreal, Flattery's stories defy genre in an affecting yet unobtrusive manner.

Readers should expect to be equal parts intrigued and unsettled." —*Publishers Weekly*

"Flattery's prose—absurd, painfully funny, and bracingly original—slingshots the stories forward. These female characters never say what you're expecting, and their insights are always incisive . . . Nervy, audacious stories in which women finally get to speak their minds."
—*Kirkus Reviews*

"With loads of strangeness, humor, and really great lines, Flattery writes women's uncanny and true lives."
—*Booklist*

"Smart as a whip, unusual, and very, very funny, Flattery's distinctive prose is a real treat."
—**Claire-Louise Bennett, author of** *Pond*

"Startling, daring, and dazzlingly dark." —**Colin Barrett, author of** *Young Skins*

"Demands repeated reading. These stories are very funny, and very sad, usually at the same time. Which, as Flattery shows us brilliantly, is the best time."
—**Jon McGregor, author of** *Reservoir 13*

SHOW
THEM
A GOOD
TIME

SHOW THEM A GOOD TIME

NICOLE FLATTERY

BLOOMSBURY PUBLISHING
NEW YORK · LONDON · OXFORD · NEW DELHI · SYDNEY

BLOOMSBURY PUBLISHING
Bloomsbury Publishing Inc
1385 Broadway, New York, NY 10018, USA

BLOOMSBURY, BLOOMSBURY PUBLISHING, and the Diana logo are trademarks of
Bloomsbury Publishing Plc

First published in 2019 in the Republic of Ireland by The Stinging Fly
First published in the United States 2020
This paperback edition published 2023

ISBN: HB: 978-1-63557-429-6; PB: 978-1-63973-073-5; EBOOK: 978-1-63557-430-2

Library of Congress Cataloging-in-Publication Data

Names: Flattery, Nicole, author.
Title: Show them a good time : short stories / Nicole Flattery.
Description: London ; New York : Bloomsbury Circus, 2019.
Identifiers: LCCN 2019041775 | ISBN 9781635574296 (hardcover) |
ISBN 9781635574302 (ebook)
Classification: LCC PR6106.L37 A6 2019 | DDC 823/.92–dc23
LC record available at https://lccn.loc.gov/2019041775

2 4 6 8 10 9 7 5 3 1

Typeset by Integra Software Services Pvt. Ltd.

Printed and bound in the U.S.A. by Berryville Graphics Inc., Berryville, Virginia

To find out more about our authors and books visit www.bloomsbury.com
and sign up for our newsletters.

Bloomsbury books may be purchased for business or promotional use. For information
on bulk purchases please contact Macmillan Corporate and Premium Sales Department
at specialmarkets@macmillan.com.

For my grandmother

There was, finally, only so much one woman on the vast and wicked stage could do.

From 'Four Calling Birds, Three French Hens'
by Lorrie Moore

Contents

Show Them a Good Time

The schemes were for people with plenty of time, or people not totally unfamiliar with being treated like shit. I was intimate with both situations. Management interviewed me – bizarre questions through an inch of plexiglass: How long, in hours, have you been unemployed? Did you misspend your youth throwing stones at passing cars?

'This can be a tangential process,' Management explained and I said sorry.

'Only peasants apologise,' Management stated and returned to her obscure markings.

The interview was an all-nighter, designed to break my spirit and ensure I pledged organisation and responsibility for the rest of my days. I emerged from it, not completely sure of anything except my own name and my age, which I knew was somewhere in my late twenties. In the morning, I was taken to the bathroom to be measured for a uniform. The toilet stall had the dark, depthless feel of a place where a body may have lain undiscovered for days. The shirt gave me breasts, the regulation boots gave me legs. All those parts I had worked so hard to forget were now reunited under surprising polyester circumstances. When I was dressed, Management offered me a manic thumbs-up. Management was round, almost perfectly so, and given to spontaneous bursts of laughter. She looked at me, at my white and empty face, and asked, 'Isn't it a great thing to be able to give yourself a giggle?' I saw in that gesture her former life as a farmhand, the crazy ease with which she sent animals off to be slaughtered.

Management explained the procedure again. Our function was to be near the till, maintain the appearance of the garage and, most importantly, *believe*. Management left the room as I screened the demonstration video. In it three participants, with the sexless good looks of catalogue models, spoke of the joy of being back at work. Whenever they did something spontaneous, or something considered outside their remit, a large X popped up on screen. As I watched I felt giddy and ashamed, as if I were witnessing a particular type of vicious pornography.

Management suggested if I ever felt like I didn't believe, I should go for a short, furious walk – maybe up and down the motorway path – and stay away from my colleagues, as my attitudes and sulky face could be hazardous. She said I seemed like a nice person and if we had customers they would probably like me. I had a personality that was best suited to short interactions.

'Should I get a business card made?' I asked.

'It's something to consider,' Management said and she repeated her manic thumbs-up.

*

Before the garage, my hometown was famous amongst people with car-sickness. It was here they stood retching and spewing before moving on somewhere better. When I came back from the city I thought we both might have changed in bright and glamorous ways, but we hadn't. We were both long acquainted with disappointment and the joys of being used.

I'd been home two months and the house felt strangely empty to me, as if all our furniture had been sold. Somehow, a hundred tiny, unspeakable events had happened in my absence. I was reunited with my mother: two flirts; two women who might find themselves in abusive relationships and not even notice; two true suckers – back together.

Every dinnertime, she questioned why I ate the way I did, why I stuck my fingers in so many jars and rooted around. Did I eat vegetables at all? Did they serve peas in many restaurants in that city? I said I didn't know, it wasn't something I thought much about, and she pointed her fork at me, that absurd vegetable speared on it, as if we shared a private joke.

'Were there boys there? Did you have a boyfriend?'

'I did.'

'Was he nice?'

'Not really. He was irritating, you know. He said things like: *I will have a small espresso.* Stuff about coffee that people already just know. He wasn't funny at all. And he kind of hit me, sometimes, in my sleep. Though I suppose I was just pretending to be asleep so it wasn't totally honest of me either.'

'It's important for a man to have a sense of humour.' A confiding, motherly smile. Her optimism was of the terrifying, impenetrable variety. It could burn through entire periods of history.

My parents had a fierce bond I admired. They had refined the habits of the long-married – saying nothing and then saying everything twice. They disregarded me, but in a practical way: the way you might ignore the weakling in a bomb shelter. Their days had their own sedate, private rhythm, punctuated by the sharp slam of the dishwasher. There was a strange, daily pattern: amble down the street; go to the supermarket; wave at a slight acquaintance; glance at the same patch of sky; come back home. They had seen boredom, stared it straight down, and survived. And still, they were less drained, less aged than I was. My father, who had always worn black, suddenly had the energy and enthusiasm for colours, and sported a pink shirt under a red golf jumper. My mother encouraged me to support his developing style. They had new friends, couples they had allegedly met in the supermarket. When these new people called on the telephone, I answered and said, 'Who is this?' and they said, 'No. *Who is this?*' like they might have stumbled across a burglary scene, a dramatic horror show that would strengthen their ties to my parents.

I lay on my lumpy bed and dreamt up inventive ways of leaving my own body. I looked down at it – slack, star-shaped – and closed my eyes, re-opened them. Still there. It didn't seem to be going away. I was restless. I made many visits to the rain barrel in the yard. I felt the rain barrel was a measure of time – all the rain collected in my two-year absence. My mother sensed the world might run out of water and this cracked, aluminium barrel was our security, our secret plan. I wanted to say, 'It's the twenty-first century,' but it sounded self-important and foreign in our hostile little house.

I had no interest in redemption. I didn't believe in it – it was for crackpots, squares – but something about that rain barrel made me want to be reborn. I could see myself sailing through the murk, the dirty leaves framing my face, the blueness of the barrel bringing out my inner Virgin Mary.

It was necessary for me to get out of the house.

*

Kevin arrived on the job exactly one week after me but immediately possessed an understanding of the garage that I lacked. He grasped its quiet romance, its rusty appeal. He knew the order we were meant to do our activities in – it was innate. I might put the mop in the bucket, or I might wring out the mop, and he would say, 'We are not supposed to do that part yet,' and he would be right. He worried about my non-linear mind but I felt we worked smoothly, as a perfect, synchronised team.

I liked him far more than was strictly encouraged. I knew Management wanted us to have a more difficult relationship, with maybe a frisson of grim sexual tension, but it didn't happen. From the beginning we shared a special atmosphere, a private connection that was pure and honest. For instance, he knew immediately whenever I was in the bathroom checking my face to see if I was still up-to-scratch, that all the waiting around hadn't ruined me. He didn't hate me for it. We both shared dim dreams of self-assertion, fantasies where we fought and emerged triumphant. We trusted each other. We made confessions. I was probably the sister he wanted to marry.

As an older woman I felt it necessary to encourage his self-esteem. I told him he looked incredible in his uniform, that it did wonders for his lanky nineteen-year-old frame. That was true. He looked like something out of a movie about bandits or serial killers on the run. Except he wasn't a bandit or a serial killer. He was the gas station attendant who pointed helpfully and said, 'They have gone that way!' He enjoyed these comparisons, these tokens.

He admitted – as we swept the garage forecourt, as we kept our eyes peeled for lucky pennies – that in his mind everything was television. There were ways of separating reality from fantasy but he did not know them. This could be a minor problem – like having trouble with directions, confusing north and south. Or it could be a major problem. Once, as we weeded the area around the rude, unnecessary fence, he told me he felt like a character being awkwardly written out of a sitcom.

'You know when they are there but they don't do or say anything? Like nobody has a clue what to do with them? Then they disappear and not a single person even bothers to mention it. That is happening to me, I think.'

I was familiar with numb feelings of this type. In the garage I felt like anyone could step in and play me, if they were supplied with the correct expression of anguish, the sluggish reactions of someone baffled by their own poor choices. Often, in the evenings, when self-pity set in, talking seemed like a good idea. I would say 'Talk to me, Kevin,' and he would oblige. Kevin's cinematic knowledge was both detailed and absurd. It left slim room in his brain for anything else, but I was grateful for it. It eased the spectral silence of the garage. I liked to make a big show of listening to him. I think it made him feel better, like he had done more than mark a time-card, weed the yard, wait.

I wanted to impress him. It was just something in the air between us.

'You know, I did some films, small parts, but I was on set.'

Both of us, perfectly unmoving in the motorway breeze.

'What was it like?' he asked.

'Like everything else after a while. Almost boring. Unpleasant. A lot of hanging around.'

'Is that why you left?'

'Yeah. And all the good roles started drying up.'

'Oh, that happens.' Kevin agreed earnestly. 'I have heard of that happening to women.'

Within a few weeks, I developed a nightly routine of walking briskly, guiltily, past the house where Kevin still lived with his father. I did not like the conclusions I came to. I could picture him inside, folded over his single bed, staring intently at a screen. Some mornings, I could imagine a faint trace of a television glow on his body.

*

It seemed embarrassing to go out looking for people I knew on my grubby, old streets, but I did it. I was past pride at this point anyway. I had put it behind me, no plans to see it again. My friends, what remained of them, were sweet girls – transparent, tame – but likeable. I assembled us together in a bar for one sorry night. Since we grew up with mothers who sat, dour, over their annual wine, we all drank like our fathers. It was our great generational decision.

Every now and then, they asked, in an offhand way, what I had done during my time away. They were furious that this was it, that they were still here, that they would never know their fully realised selves. They were ready to turn on me in a moment. In a wishy-washy attempt at sensitivity, I said that I had to leave to discover things about myself. I withheld the fact that there wasn't much to discover. Just ordinary surface and, beneath that, more desperate surface. I begged them to consider my new walk. It was a city walk. I did a demonstration. 'This is it,' I shouted as I traversed the length of their favourite and most tragic town bar.

I stressed that in the city I had worked for a number of wealthy people. I had seen my share of spectacular views because looking at things was simple and easy. I had been brought to several penthouse apartments, all of them stubbornly identical, stared out the glass and exhaled in appreciation of beauty. I took my life apart for them with a cheerful contempt. It was amusing to me.

I sensed a certain exasperation with my stories. My girls, my sweet girls, suddenly all had the searching, exhausted faces of the precariously employed. They sighed, slurped their drinks in an unladylike manner, repeated my name hundreds of times. While I had been pottering around, waiting for the right moment to introduce myself to the world, they had been attempting sombre business—trying to drink in moderation, paying motorway tolls.

Of course, we had an abrupt, jittery conversation about money. My main problem was I had none and I was uneasy about it. In the city, getting cash was no problem. Anytime I opened my purse, ugly dollars just leapt out, excited to see me. I never stole anything. I was civilised in that way. I made a living. It was a confidence trick, it was leaning in at exactly the right moment, it was lying on your back very flat, very still. Poverty was only for women who didn't know how to make slight social improvements.

My friends said I should keep busy. They were all familiar with my patterns – my fondness for just fucking things away. They had a dull list of activities for me to do. At one point or another, it was put forward, it was implied that being a good-looking person was not a full-time occupation.

'You should try it,' I said. 'Try it for a week and get back to me.'

If there was a lull in the conversation, if there was a place I could edge in, I liked to talk about the city women on the trains, the women who never removed their sunglasses. They were incredible, these ladies! They sat deathly still, their eyes shielded from the dark, metal sun and tears moving down their cheeks, as if by chance, as if it had nothing to do with them.

I exhibited much wisdom and maturity at these moments. I didn't know where it came from. I was really very drunk.

*

Back at the garage, I was in charge of the interior. It contained three tin cans of indiscernible origin, one for each shelf; a feeling of forever melancholy; a postcard of a skyscraper; and a ghostly fridge floating in the middle of the floor. We talked about painting the walls. Painting, stock, customers – Kevin had the schemes and the mindset of a helpless idealist.

As regards love and friendship, I sometimes got the sense it was a bit of a one-way street with Kevin. He was embarrassed by my cluelessness, and this brought out a red, rough rash on his cheeks and an unattractive side. I slowed him down, he said. I held him back from advancement in his field, he said. Blah-blah. He had a habit of pointing out my less-than-quick wits in the mornings. He pushed out his hands, rolled back his eyes and staggered in my direction. I was his zombie wife, his zombie sister. He added, in a polite and helpful way, that there are ways of mixing drinks so you don't get formidable hangovers.

'Don't you want this place to be nice?' he shouted at me.

'I do.' I certainly did.

'They could have given us more than three cans of godforsaken soup.'

'We don't know if they are soup.'

'What I mean is that they are not even putting in a bit of effort. In the training offices in town they have two working computers. What do we have?'

I double-tapped the postcard.

*

There was possible room for promotion at the garage and that possibility nearly drove Kevin demented. I was done with trying. There was nothing to do and I didn't feel like doing it. Just stay alive – that was my job. But Kevin was starving. Management knew just how to send him sky-high with outrageous promises and complete lack of follow-through. I said it was tacky to want to succeed at an imaginary job. I liked to be honest when I felt it was needed.

Kevin said he wished I paid the same level of care and attention to everything in the garage as I paid to the plant, which I watered daily. The plant had been introduced in the summer as a new level of responsibility. It was the sole living thing in our stockless gloom. It was green, as plants usually are, but it had a touch of the exotic about it. It was in my interest to keep it out of the sun and away from the greedy birds.

'Stop cuddling the plant,' Kevin often suggested.

'I'm just holding it,' I lied. I liked to have it in my hands, my fingers wrapped delicately around its black plastic casing. If pushed, I probably would have admitted to feeling some kind of kinship with the plant: there were hundreds of things we didn't understand about the world and there wasn't a person alive interested in telling us. Poor short and squat fellow.

Kevin blamed my passivity for our slow days. I was a human scarecrow: a strange woman, wild-haired, with end-of-the-world eyes. What town could not turn away from that? Despite his calm exterior, he was capable of great crabbiness. He screamed questions at the blameless sky. He shook the petrol pumps as if he alone could outwit their emptiness. 'We must be profitable,' he said to nobody in particular.

'Why do you move like that?' he asked once.

'It's a walk I'm trying. It's only recent. Do you like it?'

'It honestly looks like there is something wrong with you.'

'There is something wrong with me,' I said. 'When I was a child I grew at an advanced rate. My mother took me to the doctor to measure my arms and legs and they are actually two inches longer than they should be.'

I had ways of silencing Kevin, ways of forcing him to stare rigidly into the distance as if being near me required great strength. He was a young person given to habitual fits of insanity and nervy implosions. I passed several weeks simply following his erratic, slippery shadow through the glass as he stalked the garage floor. He needed to get over his moods, sharpish. But I worried about Kevin. I did. I worried about people, desperately. It took up a huge amount of my daily hours. I didn't ask to be that kind of woman but that's just the way it worked out. The reason I ended up in the garage was clear: I was being punished in a sluggish, work-shy way by the universe and, honestly, it just made me laugh.

'Why are you here, Kevin?' I asked.

'My dad said even a clown could do it.'

*

Occasionally, when people from out of town arrived in, rumpled and made frantic by too much time with

their families, I became shy. There were probably interesting things to talk about, and ways to make the garage
understood, but these people possessed an energy that
was beyond me. I was skittish, I sweated unnatural
amounts, I went unusual hues. The people moved at
a ferocious speed. They had their grand intentions –
conversation, sucky sweets, inexpensive petrol. I felt like
a child trapped in a dumb plastic playhouse before these
adults. Forever dutiful, I stuttered through my spiel:
'Thank you for visiting us today. I'm sorry I can't help
you in any way as this establishment is a participant in
the practice scheme designed to improve my skills and
eventually lead to long-term employment. I know what
you are thinking. But you would be wrong. Please take
a complimentary mint.'

The mints were my idea and I always pushed the bowl
towards the customers in what I hoped was a cordial
way. These people had a habit of looking right through
me, so it was not unusual for me to go completely
silent and turn stiffly away from them. I could still *feel*
them behind me, their impatience growing, breathing,
becoming lethal, but I never looked around. My frozen
back said it all. I returned to tending the plant or standing stupid-still with my hands resting on my thighs.
Had there been a panic button, I would have pressed
it. Kevin beamed at them as they left. Kevin said the
unique service experience dug straight into a customer's
soul. It was something to do with the correct measure of
eye contact and unobtrusiveness. Afterwards, he tended

to lock himself in the toilet stall for half an hour. He may have been punching things and missing, or not missing. I didn't know. Usually, he would emerge, in obvious despair, and accuse me of being antisocial. I was not being my premier self so he was correct in that sense.

*

Management was aggressive in her pursuit of a good time. Though she despised everything – and did unspeakable things to animals – she was, at heart, a fun-loving person. We had good times for an hour on Fridays. Kevin and I traipsed into the offices in town, where Henry and Lynn – the other two participants – were based and we all grouped semi-merrily together in the backroom. We ate supermarket-brand crisps from a cavernous bowl, electric dust coating our fingertips. We drank beers with bearded men on the labels. These men with their fishing-rods, with their broad smiles suggesting happy retirement, advised us to kick back. Have one on us. Management wanted us to be comfortable, comfortable enough to lie down playfully in each other's laps, if the desire struck us. This never once happened.

At these gatherings, it was not unusual to be offered advice that would make a 'new woman' out of me. We all agreed early on that my pretty face and nice body were my best qualities, but I could probably pull up my socks re everything else. I didn't take a whole lot of it on board. At one time or another everyone in the garage had a low opinion of me but that didn't matter so much now.

When we first met, we stood in a group circle – in my entire life, not a single good thing ever came from standing in a circle – and we introduced ourselves, announced our favourite colours and confessed to the many errors, ignorances and life missteps that had brought us here.

We listed our favourite colours in a routine way; we were careful to choose from the brighter end of the rainbow. We did not want to hint at brown, black or horrible grey deficiencies that may have resulted in termination, or some other unknown fate.

'You know what?' Management said, 'I don't have a favourite colour. I like them all. And you know what I like best?'

We made our most inquiring faces as if on the brink of revelation.

'When all the colours work together as a team.'

This was particularly popular with Lynn, our secretary of sorts from the office, who smiled effusively.

'Yes, I treat all the colours equally,' Management said, as if this were the final word on the subject.

'That's very Christian of you,' I said. Religion made me chirpy. It was so sweet and old-fashioned, like dinner and a movie.

'I don't hold any other religious beliefs,' Management blushed. 'Except I do believe in sin.'

'In that case,' I said, 'I'm not sure you are going to like what's coming next … '

There were so many words for the things I had done that it was hard to know where to start. There wasn't a single person in that backroom prepared for my shameful moments. I tried to fit as much degradation as possible into each sentence so as not to waste time. I truly wanted everyone to get their turn. I was considerate in that way. I felt, having disclosed all this information, I hadn't given myself a fair, decent start at the job, a clean slate. But, like I said, it wasn't important.

Lynn spoke about her ex-husband. The whole romance right from the get-go. I couldn't care less about whatever basement she had found the dud in, and that it had got gloomy and how they had muddled through for a while. There was a fat child born somewhere in the middle of all this, maybe? A diabetic child? I didn't know. I drifted in and out. What caught my attention was when she admitted that, during their time together, she kept a detailed record of everything her husband ate. Now, he was out there eating – at other dinner tables, at restaurants with new women – without restraint, his meals undocumented, and she was terrified. This disgusted me.

'That's not right, Lynn,' I said. 'People should be allowed to eat whatever they want without you interfering.'

Lynn really made me sick. She stormed out of the room, flying down the hall in her flat shoes. Came back a few minutes later with a puffy face. There were so many Lynns in the world, each one expecting hand-holding, mollycoddling. What to do with all of them?

Henry was here because he had limply tried to rob a post office but it was actually monstrously difficult, much more than the five-minute task he had expected. He gave up midway.

'Give 'em hell, Henry!' I commanded. I applauded any display of rebellion or wildness.

Henry had had a small, shitty life that had made waving a box-cutter in front of a few mildly frightened post-office employees seem like an empowering and enriching experience. In another better world he might have been a hero: a hairy folklore type with a soft, touchable face. Instead, he made beautifully constructed pie charts for a petrol station that did not exist.

He was beefy, mighty, capable of picking me up and swinging me around menacingly. I would shout, 'Put me down, put me down, Henry!' but not mean a word of it. It was all girlishness. I loved being picked up. Things were much clearer from that height. Despite my previous run-ins, I was still not immune to men like this.

Kevin didn't have anything to confess. He used most of his allotted time to argue for the addition of hats to our uniforms and I half fell in love with him. He became a little agitated as he tried to describe his dreams for television which, as he spoke, seemed to grow even more vague and nonsensical. The way he saw it, the problem with modern viewing was that there were too many remotes. People wanted a single, functional remote for everything and he, plaid-clad, barely pubescent, would invent it. This was an example of hope. The garage was about giving us hope. The hope of a bright future, the hope of a high tax bracket.

After the first meeting, I felt so hopeful that I went out and had seven or eight large drinks. Kevin accompanied me, my boy chaperone. We went to a godawful place I wouldn't normally be seen dead in, but it suited my state of mind at the time. The tawdry bar lights cast an angelic glow on us both. Kevin thought I drank too quickly; he put his hand over mine, said things improved if you went slow. So I drank seven or eight drinks, slowly.

'The problem is they don't *listen* to me. That's the issue at hand, Kevin,' I said.

'That's because you have literally nothing to say.'

Next day: the usual show. My bed; dry-mouthed; alone; my entire life still before me.

My mother, clad in one of my father's more colourful golf shirts, confronted me: 'I just don't think that job is bringing out the best in you.'

*

Management always found an excuse to 'pop' into the garage, wielding an enormous coffee cup along with her tremendous power. Her latest plot was to put chairs of various shapes and sizes at the front of the garage. Management had a vision of the townsfolk sitting on these chairs, chatting happily amongst themselves, and gazing luridly at their young people as they busied themselves being employed. It was as if the chairs could sense the unreasonable expectations placed upon them; they vomited their stuffing, revealed dangerous wooden splinters, and discoloured horribly in the daylight.

During the chair-moving task I did my best to be well-mannered, uninventive, kindly.

'The weather is cold today,' I once offered.

'Only idiots talk about the weather,' Management replied as she surveyed me from a sinister distance.

I tried to leave a baffling number of times. Each time I tucked my hair behind my ears in a nod towards a tidy aesthetic and squeezed myself into Management's tiny cubicle. 'I quit. Thank you,' I'd say and Management would reply, 'I will see you tomorrow,' and somehow she was right and I was always destined to be wrong.

*

I had up-and-down periods. I experienced great bursts of tenderness towards Kevin, the pigeons that littered the garage forecourt, even the empty chairs. I was hugely nostalgic and wistful for the garage even while I was still technically working there.

'Kevin, do you remember the good times we used to have?'

He looked at me. 'Not really.'

Then: the anxious darkness, a rising feeling that I might rip all the leaves from the plant for no good reason, an anticipated anger at the next person who might dare touch me.

'I hate this place and if you are having similar feelings, my friend, we should run away,' I said.

'Haven't you just come back from running away?'

The garage encouraged education – learning skills that would be transferable to newer, better positions – and in its own sterile way, it succeeded. I gained insights into my own personal habits that I could have gone decades quite happily never knowing about. This mental unravelling happened at no great speed. Even the catastrophe of my own life was something I managed with amazing slowness.

*

Christmas came from nowhere. 'When was that decided?' I wanted to ask, but it brought a new thrill and direction to our days so I didn't want to argue. Management, occupying the head chair, her smooth, superior hands sitting on the table, searched out themes for the decorating. And in a burst of friendliness and participation, that surprised even myself, I suggested we went with 'Christmas'.

'In what way?' Management inquired.

'You know the festive way with tinsel and the colour red?'

She pursed her woeful, shrivelled lips.

'Can you not think of anything else?'

'No.'

In that brief moment everyone saw my mind and my mind was absent of all ideas. I thought I would be a different person by this time in my life, but I was actually becoming less like someone else and more like myself. It was troubling. Kevin ignored me during that

Christmas discussion. Often, during Friday group, he sat across from me with Henry and Lynn. I tried to let him know we were being held hostage using just my eyes but I could widen them only so far to convey the corniness, the stupidity. I sometimes saw him laugh with his hand over his mouth – that was for me.

'Don't give out to her just because she didn't have a good theme,' said Lynn with deft and hidden savagery. She was the kind of woman who would cause tears in others just to wipe them away. Lynn had no respect for complicated people and situations. It was so lousy and exhausting. It probably had caused a lot of problems in her life. And she was brutal at her job. She made *me* look conscientious. She simply had to draft email correspondence, but she never quite got the tone right; there was always a whiff of incompetency. We were all nervous about her genuine ineptitude. I, for example, was consumed by compassion for her child.

'I'm not giving out to her,' Management said.

'Good, because you know she's not all there.'

'Why isn't she all there?' Henry piped up, in a rare moment of conversation.

'On account of all, the, you know … ' Lynn whispered.

'What was that, Lynn?' I said.

She looked directly at me. 'You know,' she repeated, stiffly.

'No,' I said. 'I forget. Please tell me.'

'You were,' she cleared her throat delicately, 'a fantasy girl.'

'The pornography,' Management stated, flatly. 'The prostitution.'

'And that's just the stuff she has told us about.' Lynn shook her head sadly. 'It was a lot of work for me, you know, a lot of extra work for me. When I was doing up our history folders on the computer, I had no idea what to call hers. I stayed late. I couldn't figure it out.'

'What did you go with in the end?' Management inquired.

'Whoring Around.'

'That's a powerful title for a folder, Lynn,' Management congratulated her. 'You're really improving at the computer.'

'Don't hold back, you two,' I said. 'Pretend I'm not here.'

Kevin's sly smile.

'Can we all try and enjoy ourselves please?' Management's voice was sharp, high with that animal bloodlust.

We nodded. Our heads bobbing, bobbing, bobbing.

Management was not above demeaning us. She had lofty, liberal ideas but she was as base as anyone I have ever encountered. She disguised it as fun and games – playtime – but it was tyranny. Pure, intentional terror. There had been ugly scenes in the past. Things had gotten nasty, once or twice.

That Friday, she took out a small cardboard box and placed it on the table in front of her.

'Can you come up here, Kevin?'

Kevin lumbered towards her and as she rested one hand on his queasy, young shoulder she pressed an object into his palm.

At the sight Kevin's whole body clammed up; he disappeared into himself. I caught only a flash of it – the sorrow, the roundness, the honking redness. As Kevin stretched that clown nose over his startled face, the silence in the backroom was clammy, damp.

'Isn't it amusing?' Management asked.

'It's brilliant,' I said. 'May I have one please?'

'The nose is just for Kevin.'

'I would like one.'

'Don't be a sourpuss.'

'Just give me one, would you?'

'Why?'

'Because it would look fucking good on me.'

Management rolled her eyes, weighed up something in her mind and, finally, threw me the prop. I placed it over my face in what I hoped was a demonstration of anger.

'Now, isn't this a nice evening?' Lynn said.

*

The next morning I came to on Kevin's couch, his *Jaws* T-shirt stretched foolishly over my chest, the shark slithering up to say hi. I could taste the night before – the emotion, the dramatics. My impassioned speeches left highly irregular tastes. Through the kitchen wall came the low murmur of television, accompanied by the mean movements of Kevin's full-time bastard of a father.

Fridays were not easy on Kevin either, make no mistake. After the meetings he frequently had dreams where he chased me off a cliff.

*

At the Christmas party, Kevin and I were both rewarded with a bottle of Chardonnay. I think we were supposed to be awed, or at least grateful. Back at the garage, we strung handfuls of fairy lights around the plant. I placed the star, sideways, on top. All lit up like a Christmas tree, that old story. We sat heavily on the spotless floor, mixed our drinks in paper cups, and watched the motorway opening and closing in front of us like an accordion.

'You never know, Kevin, you might get laid in the stationery cupboard.'

'We don't have a stationery cupboard.'

'That was a joke.'

'Didn't Management warn you about those?'

I liked Kevin's sincerity, his skinny torso, his rancid, red-light district aftershave. I was fond of it all. It had nothing to do with his looks – which were limited – or where he lived, or if he was interesting and successful in a way that was supposed to appeal to me. Nowadays, you have to be careful who you fall for, but I liked Kevin. He didn't ask anything of me. That wasn't nothing. If it was, more people would have done it.

'Don't worry,' I said. 'You won't get laid. You are weird and flat-broke.'

'Ah.' He took a swift drink. 'But so are you.'

I nodded, my expression grave. 'That is correct, Kevin. Very clever of you to notice that.'

*

The first person to occupy a seat on the garage forecourt was a local man in his late seventies. He arrived in early January, wore a three-piece suit and leaned heavily on a gnarled cane, like a guest from another era. He was harmless, his own deterioration driving him out of his house and into the world. I thought he sat on the high stool with a magnificent dignity, his back resting on the chain-link fence.

'Keeping busy?' he shouted at me across the forecourt.

I waved my arms around in a demonstration of busyness. 'Yes, yes, I am.'

'Nothing like it. Great to see it.'

'Thank you.'

'I hear you were away?'

'I was.'

'What did you do over there?'

I shrugged. 'Nothing good.'

'Well, you are back now and you are doing a fine job. Stay at it.'

Sometimes his wife came with him. They'd hobble down the motorway path together, so tiny, so diminished, they almost disappeared. Each time, they brought me strange gifts that I suspected they found on the roadside: a scratched CD of affectionate love songs, a silvery disco jacket for a Barbie.

'But I don't own a doll?'

'Consider it a present,' his crinkly wife winked. She was maybe deaf.

Whenever Management appeared, the old man liked to bellow and point.

'That's a great girl you have there!'

Management always spun around rapidly, fiercely, like she was in a cop show, hoping to find a new, normal person. But, no – it was just me.

We were both equally surprised.

*

At night, the garage often welcomed other, less accommodating visitors. Young men who stepped out from behind the wheels of their tin cans like small, showy princes. They all drove cars that looked like they were designed to be in accidents – scraps of metal with a colony of screaming girlfriends trapped inside. I squirmed at their clumsy, implied intimacy.

Was I always this quiet?

I was.

Did it not get boring?

No, not ever.

I was careful not to move during these conversations – I did not want to draw attention to myself even though I was on display. They had caught some of the films I had been in and you know what? I wasn't nearly as hot in real life.

I was scum, trashy, that was the word, repulsive. Et cetera. They called me other names too. Wholly unimaginative stuff. Plain lazy.

Then there were others, who were worse. Smart and careful – they made assumptions. From whatever they had learned in college, they were concerned my self-esteem might be on the lower end of the spectrum. I said, 'Of course, I have low self-esteem. You think I would be standing here talking to you if I didn't?'

I entertained one or two of them, those who made a true first impression: new disasters. I liked conversation and challenging situations. If they pushed me, I pushed right back. Why not? I bit down hard on my bottom lip. There was blood drawn, but it didn't bother me. I promised myself this would all end, at some point or another.

Many took greedy fistfuls of mints before they screeched off. I had to get Kevin to watch the till as I refilled the bowl. I had to be alone. I needed to rub my hand across my mouth and face while comforting myself with scenarios: telephone poles springing from hallowed ground, hard, unforgiving walls stretching soundlessly across the motorway, bodies thrown into the starless night.

I wasn't feeling good about myself. I wasn't feeling relaxed and it showed.

One evening, Kevin approached me with the bare and battered plant. His voice was not far from tears. 'What happened?'

I looked at the plant. 'We had a falling out.'

I returned to rearranging the chairs, my freckled back sadly exposed.

*

More and more people began drifting into the garage forecourt on a daily basis to watch Kevin and me. These 'customers' had no single defining characteristic; they were fuzzy, unfamiliar. It was as if Kevin and I blinked them in and out of existence. The garage was not our place anymore. Often, the strangers feigned indifference but their eyes followed us, their gazes alert as we performed. I was not aware my town had people like this. Middle-aged bodies in stretched jeans, with sharp, angry jaws. They rarely sat, instead they loitered around the chairs, exuding a dangerous energy. Occasionally, they made pointing motions, fraught signals as if guiding Kevin and I across the garage forecourt. Sometimes, they clapped their hands against their knees and cheered us on.

Management advised us to engage with them and I did. I asked questions like: 'Is my hair nice pushed back?' and 'What have I done to deserve this life?' I came back to life in their presence, was strangely reassembled as a homely hostess, with her hands spread wide open. I did not know who I was fooling, them or me.

But Kevin wilted. His eccentricities were very apparent under the strangers' constant supervision. He was inelegant. I slicked back his hair with foul-smelling gel and tucked in his shirt. It didn't help. All this time, I thought he was just an ordinary loser but it was worse than that. The people disliked him. Anytime he wandered onto the garage forecourt, the people looked away. While he worked, some even turned their chairs to face the opposite direction, like the garage was a stage and Kevin was a character they refused to acknowledge.

*

'What was it like seeing yourself onscreen?' he asked one day. 'Was it scary?'

'It was incredible,' I said casually. 'I mean there was a lot going on in the scenes I was in, a lot of distracting stuff. But I looked great.'

'I'm sure,' Kevin said, and he pretended to be suddenly invested in a balloon.

'It was amazing. I could have been anyone, anyone at all.'

'That must have been hard,' he said.

Kevin always missed the point. That was going to be an obstacle for him, going forward.

'No, Kevin,' I said. 'Being anyone was the entire appeal.' The garage was not real but it was still the most real experience I'd had in years. In the city, my boyfriend was the director, but he was no artist. He didn't have that sort of intelligence. All he knew was how to fuck people over, drink infinite blue cocktails, and make everything cheap. I had more vision than him. I had a lot of excellent suggestions for set design, but I kept them to myself. Trapped in our smooth apartment, in our terrible bedroom, I trained myself to sleep for only four hours a night. I had to be prepared to jump up and raise my fists to the dead night. It was so pathetic, it didn't suit him at all.

Usually when he was halfway through hitting me it would occur to him just how obvious he was. Then he would curl up, say sorry, baby, sorry, sorry. Baby this, baby that, baby all the livelong day. It was possible that this person who owned me didn't even know my name. It was all a dull attempt to get my attention, and the stuff he bought me was dog-ugly. He got it into his head that I was kitsch and he just went with it without my permission. He gave me one pair of costly pants meant for 'leisure'. I wore them outside – they were okay pants – and this was a big no-no, apparently. 'They are only for leisure!' Those kind of rules. It was hard to know who to be minute by minute.

His friends were in the films too and I just put on a wig, let them do whatever they wanted to me, went home, practised falling asleep and then leaping awake. It killed time. After that, there was emptiness. Some wandering around, eating not-good stuff out of bags, doughnuts, Taco Bell. Enough loneliness to make you lose your mind. I got my nails done twice a week – there was a violence to it that I worshipped. The rooms where I was filmed were just like beauty parlours: the same glossies on the coffee tables, the same plastic furniture, nothing words snapping into the air. Girls, lots of them – all of us mutely conspiring, an exclusive club.

I spent the last two months of our relationship staring straight past my boyfriend's head. I played a lot of

Candy Crush. It was just easier for everyone that way. I was such a good girlfriend, god damn it. It was an outrage how lovely I was. I was the very best until the morning, the morning that came from nowhere, when I woke up and said, 'I'm going home.' He just rolled over onto his side, gave me a filthy look like I was quitting, slipping out early. His last words to me: 'Don't misrepresent the company.'

'How did you get into it?' Kevin asked. He was doing his version of eye contact.

I shrugged. 'Well, I'd gone all that way. I had to do something.'

*

On the first day of a freezing spring, I came in to find the light not working and Kevin absent. I loitered. I hung around late, scuffing the concrete, flicking bits of dirt from under my fingernails. He did not arrive the following day either, although I stood at a visible point on the motorway path waiting for him. I consulted the strangers, gazed into their flat, flavourless eyes, and they adopted innocent faces, like they had nothing to do with this disaster. Some displayed befuddlement at the mention of Kevin's name. Others just laughed. It wasn't confusing – it was the opposite. It was the first moment that made sense.

From that day forth, I decided to stay safely inside the garage. I swaddled myself in Kevin's old sweatshirt and made advancements for us both. I consulted interior decorating magazines; I recognised all the women who posed languidly over chairs. I pushed the fridge to one end of the garage, using all my body weight and will. I unscrewed an overhead light bulb, held its cold glass in my hand, crushed it, threw the shards out the window and watched them fly towards the strangers. I told myself that when the lights went back up, everything would be different. I lit dozens of candles and left them in precarious places. I didn't cry but, if it had happened, I would have allowed it. On the garage forecourt, I only appeared once or twice and that was to chase away the pigeons. I charged out into the fog and dirt, deliberately angry and ugly. I wanted these people to know that Kevin was capable of great, complicated feelings, and they had done something to him, something awful, and I did not like it.

Management arrived when I was sitting beside the fridge, in flattering candlelight, my fingers resting on my lumpy knees. She had heard of the temporary changes I had made to the garage and she expressed concern. She said that she couldn't help but notice at the last Friday meeting that I wasn't really there, my name had to be called at least three times before I snapped to attention. She hunkered down beside me, kindly, as if preparing me for bad news. Her body was uncomfortably close to mine: a body I did not want to know a single thing about.

'Can I have Kevin back please?'

I hated how wanting I sounded.

'Kevin wasn't panning out. He received a fine severance package.'

I glanced at the shelves and noticed where there were once three cans, there were now only two.

*

There were things happening out there in the world – history, events. But history was not happening in my town, not to me. I was just standing outside bars, without my coat, shoes and underwear, wondering where exactly they were because – sadly – I was not wearing them. My thoughts had reached a manic, fever pitch. I had taken to becoming a resigned passenger in cars that traversed the motorway; these were meaningless trips but I did not sleep well after them. I watched my old films on my phone, my legs curled up underneath me, my heart beating fast. All those devastating angles. I wanted them to be instructional, but they told me nothing about myself. I got weary simply fast-forwarding through them. The furniture was always wrong.

I watched early CCTV footage of Kevin and me, both of us sauntering around, looking oddly delighted in our own misery. It was amazing how little we did. I regretted not laying down in his lap when Management encouraged it; that was my true regret. I wondered when he knew it was his final shift, before or afterwards. I genuinely hoped it was after. I imagined myself, barefoot, sprinting down the motorway path after him.

I resolved to replace the light bulb and that became my daring project. With Henry's assistance, I took a stepladder from the office in town and practised climbing up and down the three steps. I had never replaced a light bulb before. It was difficult work. I must have walked to the hardware shop, I must have put one achingly slow foot in front of the other, but I have no recollection of doing so. Suddenly, I was just there. I spent hours picking the perfect one; I had experience in the right wattage and what it could do for a scene. In the light bulb's reflection, I was stretched and distorted to a stunning degree. On my way out, I heard the cashier advise a young lady to be careful while doing home renovations, but this did not apply to me.

*

On the day of the light bulb replacing, I felt an exciting charge like I was revved up. It was a special day, no doubt. I knew this because at the front door of the garage a new plant greeted me – a first-place pageant bow running around its black casing, its leaves in full bloom – a gift with no note, celebrating nothing.

'Oh good,' I said. 'You got here just in time.'

I did not want to rush the task. I propped up the plant nearby to keep a close eye on me. I needed to take it easy, slow. It was important. I was a long way from the ground. I tried to steady myself while saying,

'Woah, woah'. I caught only the bright tip of the wire as the ladder slipped from underneath me. And as I went hurtling through, all the way through the cement floors, everything – everything – looked familiar and enchanting.

Sweet Talk

All that summer, the flies were an irritation. They disturbed our dinners so we erected a fly-catcher, a bright sticky orange strip that displayed the lurid corpses. My father told me I swallowed them at night; they travelled down my throat and settled in my stomach. In the mornings, before my preening routine, I examined my mouth for evidence of badness – black stains on the bottom of my teeth, a broken wing lodged under my tongue.

The men lived in the caravan. They arrived in threes – mute, unfriendly, unsmiling – and it was my mother's job to let them know when they were finished. My father would say to her, 'Get that done,' and she would set off across the lawn. If she liked the men, if she had spoken to them or they had been in the house, she took the time to compose a personal letter – her childish scrawl offering basic commiserations. If she did not have any sense of them she simply said, 'Boys, get your belongings.'

My father used any excuse to sack them. He disliked evidence of effort, and he abhorred vanity in men. He considered it unnatural. He resented these sullen strangers, the suggestion of wax in their hair, their good complexions. Usually, he didn't even bother to learn their names. As unceremoniously as they arrived, they made their way down the gravel drive. Some had suitcases, or large backpacks; others carried their things in plastic bags. I watched their departures from my bedroom window as it seemed important – becoming acquainted with men's disappointed backs, watching their retreating shadows.

That summer, the summer I turned fourteen, was warm. We had no language for the weather. We wandered around like people burdened and we pointed at the sky. The missing women of the Midlands peered out of the papers; their vague and vanished faces seemed to understand the tedium of the heat. The women had all disappeared from nothing places. It was a long walk into town from our house, a town with a heavy thrum of dark traffic. I did that walk daily, sometimes wearing shoes, sometimes not. I had adopted a uniform of flimsy halter-strap tops and pedal pushers with beads oddly, and uncomfortably, attached to the cuffs. I brushed my hair out and made necklaces from multi-coloured rope. People asked if I was a hippie and I said, yeah, I was.

I was happy for the break from school – I had become too good at being who I was. When one of the more established girls gave a blow job beside the Virgin Mary statue outside the school, I declared myself unimpressed by the obvious symbolism and others followed suit. I had a quiet sort of pull in that way. There was speculation that I might have significant breasts underneath my school jumper, but it was not a card I would be playing so it didn't warrant much discussion. There were faint rips in our universe – the missing girls, the blow job – but nothing ever ruptured in the way we wanted it to. We sowed pleats into our skirts to make them tighter, we snapped our hair into humourless ponytails. That summer, we watched scary movies we selected brazenly from the back of the video shop. At night, our film minds whirring, we fell asleep with our hands on the small of each other's backs.

At the edge of our town, a new housing estate was built – the first of many – and it brought with it a sense of novelty. There were boys in those cheaply built houses, boys who had to move schools, boys who had hurriedly left cities, and we all lied to each other about our levels of experience. The three-beds faced an area of stubby, patchy grass and the boys called it the green. We always split up according to some hierarchy I couldn't fathom and I was left with the quietest, the kindest, the one who had spent the least amount of time in a juvenile detention centre. He would pull down my bra-strap, pull it back up, pull it back down as if to say: Nope, I have no idea what's happening here either.

In the evenings, when my friends and I were alone, we talked about the missing girls. We admitted we thought some of them were plain.

Before the Australian arrived, the missing girls were the main priority. They had been sucked into a blood-red sky, summoned into a gaping, flame-filled ground. The man who took them was Freddy Krueger, his claw-hand stretching out of a silent car, skirting slender upper arms. We dripped ice cream onto our laps, our bare stomachs. The girls said 'Candyman' three times into an unforgiving mirror. We sat on walls, we skipped through side alleys. We sauntered around, bare-shouldered, waiting for cars to beep at us, seeking any tiny confirmation that we were alive.

My mother, threatened by the modernity of the new estate, had decided to gut the kitchen. The Australian was recommended to my father by a friend, but it was clear from the start that he didn't know what he was doing. His talents extended to drawing elaborate sketches of a wood-panelled kitchen, but no further. He pored over these squiggles with a look of wild concentration, but resisted doing anything as serious as actual physical labour. My father liked him in the way that men who don't say much often do like each other. He was rewarded with a key to the caravan and my father insisted that once he got started on the farm – once he settled in – he would be an excellent worker. The kitchen project was abandoned, as my mother always knew it would be.

He was in his early thirties and if you didn't know him, you would have presumed him to be stupid. He had one of those unlucky faces that could so easily be described as slack-jawed, and a great braying laugh. He also had a sad, lazy way of confirming people's low expectations of him. On good days, he was a charming stranger. Other days, he was simply the man who stood squinting in our yard. His clothes were not well cared for – a button missing, a shirt cuff frayed or torn, the material faded in places from the sunlight. He had no passions, nothing he talked about with enthusiasm. It takes a special kind of hard-working mind to fall for someone so helplessly and honestly ordinary.

'I'm in love,' I announced to my mother, refusing to elaborate.

I had a babysitting job in the next town over, something I'd acquired in an effort to overthrow my parents. The Australian collected me each night in my father's filthy car and I endured five-minute journeys that felt like actual physical suffering. I baffled myself with the blandness of my own conversation. I inquired about the length of the train trips he had taken around Europe. Did he have a normal cabin or a night cabin? Did they serve food on board? Was it fast?

My friends and I had idle thoughts that we should be elsewhere – at the small, mean local summer camps, perhaps, improving ourselves – but we dismissed them. If feeling energetic, we entertained the idea of tennis – but only the idea of it. We ran and scattered, ran and scattered. We rehearsed, again and again, the stories of the missing girls. We sketched love hearts on our skin with sun cream. We were always projecting futures: we were dropping out of school, we were going to live in caravans, raise our children collectively with few rules. On my fourteenth birthday, we went to the one pub that allowed us in and leaned across the pool table like we were working for tips.

One night, collecting me, the Australian caught sight of my friends and I could see him appraising their outfits and sly, knowing gaits.

'Those girls will get you into trouble,' he said.

I shrugged like I couldn't wait.

(He was right. In three years, at exam-time, I would be dragged into an airless room, papers would be flung at me, and a nun would say, Well, things aren't looking so amusing now, are they? It's a shame, the nun would say, because when you came into this school we thought you were going to do great things. Now, we would be surprised if you do anything – anything at all. And, not for the last time in my life, I would curse myself for laughing when nothing was funny, and staying still when I should have been moving, and moving when I should have been staying still.)

If my parents went out, he was instructed to call to the main house to check on me. They were meant to be brief visits but time always got away from us; two people aware they were doing something wrong but not knowing how to name it. One evening, I begged him to stay and watch *The Exorcist*. As an incentive, I offered microwave pizza.

'Are you old enough?' he asked, referring to the film.

'Yes,' I said, disgusted.

The film was dark, but I thought it would be darker, more twisted. It was just priests, really – priests in unusual circumstances.

He yawned and leaned back on the leather couch, revealing a large scar running from the top of his trousers to his belly-button, healed but still red and angry-looking. I glanced and he pulled down his T-shirt. 'What are you scared of?' he asked me.

'Nothing,' was what I wanted to say, but I had some-how got it into my head that it was wrong to lie to the people you love. So I told him – I knew the way I talked with my friends was silly, that the man who took the missing girls didn't have a hook for a hand. He was prob-ably normal, and you would be an idiot if you believed otherwise. And that's how it would be forever – the people who hurt us would look normal and be normal, except for the one thing that meant they weren't.

'They are some interesting thoughts for a thirteen-year-old girl,' he said.

'Fourteen,' I corrected him.

I slid closer to him on the couch and thought about how his hands would feel underneath my clothes. Onscreen, the actress spewed and I explained it was pea-soup. I wanted him to understand that you could fool other people but you couldn't fool me.

*

We read aloud an article from a woman's magazine and giggled. 'In her lifetime, a woman will have an average of twelve lovers.' Twelve seemed an extraordinary number to us then. What would we say to all these men? What would we say to them with our clothes off? We thought about the missing girls. How many boyfriends did they have before they were taken? One? None?

He invited a woman to stay with us and, unbelievably, she did. Her named was Genevieve. He didn't call her his girlfriend, but he didn't have to. It was my first encounter with jealousy and I took a lively interest in it. Out of solidarity, so did my friends. Together we hated her with all the blackness we could muster. We hated her haircut, which we suspected was a pudding-bowl style but spiked up. A secret pudding-bowl. We hated her long, thin legs which she paraded in shorts. We hated the colourful silk underwear she hung up to dry outside the caravan. This underwear was so obviously corrupt that we wondered if there was an authority figure we could contact about it? What did it cover? Where could you buy it? We hated her Australian accent and her expression of gentle, calm acceptance. When the boys from the green asked about her – they had seen her striding through town – we nearly lost our minds with outrage. She was ancient. She was twenty-four.

I rifled through her things, her creams and lotions, as though, if carefully handled, they could reveal her secrets to me. I had become an expert at this scandalous practice from babysitting for a family who paid me very little, or sometimes paid me in chocolate, or, most usually, didn't pay me at all. I quietly ripped apart their home as if it were a formal duty. I studied receipts, flicked tiredly through their clothes, checked out the hidden corners of their bedside lockers. If I took something, I felt no guilt about it. I told myself it was because they were blow-ins, because they had more money than my family, because they had lived. Or I told myself these small items would prefer to come with me, that I could give them a better home.

The parents were oddly faceless to me. They trusted me with their child, when they probably shouldn't have. He ran around the house naked, shrieking, exposing his nubby penis, and I did little or nothing to stop him. I often hid in the hope that my disappearance and dramatic reappearance would calm him. Or I closed my eyes and wished that when I re-opened them he would simply be gone. This worked once, and when it did, my body shut down. I ran through the house, wearing new shorts that felt grim and foolish, shouting his name. Eventually I found him outside, playing happily in the patch of land they called the green.

That night, on the drive home, mistaking my terror for sensitivity, the Australian complimented me on my silences. He said most people didn't know when to be quiet. I agreed and I huddled closer to the car door. I couldn't tell him I had magicked away a child, that I was evil, that my legs looked squat in shorts. Passing under the eerie streetlights, on the blank roads, we looked like a photograph from an instructional pamphlet warning about the dangers of strange men. Or the dangers of babysitters. Or the greatest pamphlet never written: a warning of the romantic danger of being left alone in a car with someone you're attracted to.

A willing silence working in my favour, he said, 'Genevieve wants me to marry her.'

I suspected that she had followed him here with that in mind. I often found her looking disagreeably at the notice board in the supermarket, picking up signs for gardening jobs or part-time secretarial work, and putting them down again.

'People like to do that,' I said, as if I had already dismissed marriage as an option for myself.

'Should I?' he smiled the useless, halting smile of the perennially uncertain. He looked at me, urgent, as if it was a decision we could reach together.

'You should do whatever you want,' I told him.

I had been measured for a bra recently and my breasts were actually largish. We were probably going to start going to discos soon. I owned several skirts. I would be fine.

Genevieve's problem was she came to Ireland looking for her boyfriend, the one she met at home, but he was gone. He had changed. 'Big deal,' I said to my mother. We all had stuff going on. 'Big deal,' my mother promised. 'Until it happens to you.'

Genevieve hung around the main house, snacking, exchanging tips for lined eyes with my mother. Her presence only confirmed what I'd always known about my mother – she would have been a different sort of woman if my father and I had let her. My father and I had something definite in common that didn't even need to be mentioned, and we excluded her. In that hot, rotting kitchen, the flies conspiring above our heads, my mother talked to Genevieve about her life as though it was still a work in progress. She spoke condescendingly of the people in the town, as though they were characters in a book she had picked up and quickly put down, bored. It was unnerving. One more week with Genevieve and I think my mother would have lost all inhibitions, and said: 'You know what? I hate this dump and every last person living in it.' There were several things I couldn't bear to hear and that was top of the list.

We felt sure Genevieve wouldn't last until the end of the summer, but she confounded even us with how quickly she left. I watched her outside the caravan most nights and, despite myself, I felt pity for her. She sat in an old deckchair, smoked roll-ups and sang quietly, holding slight notes. She drank beer and let the bottles roll away from her. I had never heard songs like that before, they weren't rock songs or songs off the radio, and she never knew all the words.

If she was waiting for him to come out and join her, he never did. Her last week they fought loudly and frequently. Her face developed the sunken look of someone who has become familiar with saying sorry.

This was it, according to my mother, the only story – the woman behaved desperate, got it in the neck, went ugly. He took her bag to the front gate, but didn't wait with her. I asked her if she had a plan and she said, God, no, I don't have a fucking clue where I'm going, and that answer seemed brave and insane all at once. My friends and I celebrated her departure like it was an amazing heist we had pulled off. We went to the pub and got ambitious with alcohol left in abandoned glasses. It made us solemn. Genevieve was tall and the right age. She had good legs. We hoped she didn't hitch.

Shortly after she left, my mother came into the bathroom when I was in the tub and sat on the edge. I pulled my knees up. Our bath was cracked and plastic and, if I splashed, water flooded the floor, soaked into the hallway, trickled into the kitchen and someone, it didn't matter who, screamed.

'Was Genevieve pregnant, do you think?' she asked me.

This was how it was with my mother – everyone was either pregnant or dying.

'No,' I said and dipped the tendrils of my hair into the water. I watched them floating shapelessly like weeds. 'Not pregnant,' I said, preoccupied. 'Just annoying.'

(At sixteen one of us would become pregnant. Statistics dictated it would be one of us and statistics will have their dreary way.)

A man was caught violating a woman in a car, not far from us. The woman escaped. The man became a suspect in the missing girls and we gathered around our parents' leftover papers. Violating, we agreed, was a funny, old-fashioned word. When they questioned this man, he said of the escaped woman, 'She's lucky: she's alive.' We widened our wild eyes at each other, still brave then, still merciless. Can you believe that, we repeated? She's lucky: she's alive.

The summer slipping away from me, I went to the caravan. He wasn't there but the lights were on and I let myself in. It was damp and musty and had the air of everything being put together in a hurry. The duvet cover was from an old set I recognised from my parents' room. There wasn't an oven, just a hotplate with a tube linking it to a canister of gas outside. There was barely anything hanging on the clothing rail. No photos, no postcards. I thought he would revert back to himself, happy again, after Genevieve left, but the opposite happened. He kept odd hours, stayed up all night and returned from the fields in the mornings rumpled, smiling manically. He made mistakes with the animals. He bought a pack of cards and let me beat him, howling mockingly at the moon. He touched my face, told me I was a good girl.

In the bathroom, Genevieve's creams still littered the shelves as a reminder of her. My intention hardened when I saw them. I sat opposite the slim sliver of wardrobe mirror. I had a babyish face that no amount of make-up could transform. I removed my top. I took off my trousers too and I was, surprising myself, in my underwear. My bra and pants were gritty, cheap and childish looking so I took them off too. It was cold because the window was not a proper window, just two boards my mother had nailed up.

Outside, I could hear the familiar creak of the deck-chair and I knew he had arrived back. There was the short snap of matches being lit one after the other. I felt something fluttering on my back teeth. I reached right in, all the way into the part of my mouth I did not know, and yanked out a trail of dead flies – black, long and sticky-looking. I discarded them and I waited.

Hump

At seventy, after suffering several disappointments, the first being my mother, the second being me, my father died. One evening he gathered the family in his room and asked if anyone had any questions. No one did. The next day he died. At the funeral everyone looked like someone I might sort of know. These strangers told anecdotes and made general health suggestions to each other. I passed out the sandwiches. The sandwiches were clingfilmed and oddly perforated, like they had been pierced again and again by cocktail sticks. I said 'Sambo?' to every single person in that room. It was a good word, a word I hoped would get me through the entire evening. I wasn't strong on speaking or finding ordinary things to discuss in large groups. The place was crowded with false grief, people constantly moving positions, like in A & E, depending on the severity of their wounds. I mentioned that I held his wrist when he passed and through the use of the phrase 'flickering pulse' I was booted up to First Class.

My father told me he regretted not talking more. He felt the time others used for conversation, he had filled with snooker or nodding or looking away. He surmised, through a mouthful of diabetic chocolate, that he had only spoke thirty per cent of his life. It was a dismal percentage and I was familiar with what dismal percentages could do to a person. We were spending a lot of time together then, linking arms and being totally happy. I had this one trick I did for him. I'd curl up tight into his bed, under the starched sheets, and peep out at the nurses like I was an old lady. It was a scream. They said I was their youngest patient. I laughed and asked them to leave the pills in a tidy arrangement on the bedside locker. My antics gained me a certain level of recognition and infamy in the retirement home and, at times, I could feel my father almost bursting with pride. We both agreed it was the perfect trick for the occasion of his near-death.

I was good at gestures, but it was only in that function room when I spoke my sad-but-true stories in my fragile tone that I finally got the appeal of talking. I thought this is what I will be now: a talker. My career had taken a sinister turn and I had started to keep an eye out, like you do for a new lover, for other things I could try. There weren't many. All jobs seemed to contain one small thing I just could not do. It was maddening.

I told a number of stories about my father that evening. I was there, but I wasn't. My mind was mainly preoccupied with what I could do in my new life as a talker: I would be both stylish and intelligent but also deeply affecting in

my conversation. When that room of strangers looked up
at me I did not know if I wanted them to cry or to clap.

It was in the shower where I found it first. I had moved
into my father's old house, and sometimes would shower
sitting down on the stool that was installed for comfort
or, if I was feeling up to it, I would stand. The bathroom
was filthy with intermittent flashes of what looked like the
colour peach. On sitting-down days, I often crawled from
one side of the room to the other. I could get away with
this because I lived alone. It must have been a standing
day as I realised I was a lot closer to the taps than I used to
be. I was a lot closer to the hair on the taps. I was stooping
over like I was playing the Old Lady in a celebrated stage
production, except I was all scrunched up and very naked.
I pressed my fingers below my shoulders and felt it shift-
ing, unfurling. The hard roundness of it – like a golf ball
or a marble. I dressed myself quickly, being careful not to
catch sight of it in the mirror. When I stood on the train
that morning, my fingers gripping the rail above, I could
feel it growing beneath my skin like a second layer of flesh.

I worked in an office outside the city and we all had
the appearance of people who had been brutally exiled.
We shed our city selves but, lacking imagination, we
had nothing to replace them with. Between the forty
of us, I think we could have made a complete person.
I had been there six months and it was probably the
longest position I ever held. None of it mattered but
I liked to pretend it did. If someone came in, I might

say 'Come in!' That was it. That was the whole script. It wasn't exactly spiritually fulfilling. Often, I was so bored I couldn't hold a conversation. I walked around cubicles abandoning sentences. Whenever I entered the kitchen area, my colleagues left quickly and without warning. I think they were jealous because my desk got the most direct sunlight. I didn't understand them at all. I had a habit of thinking I was very unique and interesting.

My one friend spent her days on the phone to the refuse collection. There had been a dispute over the bins, no one knew who started it, but the rubbish had not been collected in six weeks and it was not a time for chit-chat, idle or otherwise. I wanted to tell Paula about my discovery, ask her had she noticed anything different about me, but all she did was place her hand over the mouthpiece of her phone and mutter 'Sorry'. She had married young and was squeamish about all sorts.

I used my mornings to investigate what was wrong with me. I opened several internet tabs, each one containing something possibly wrong, and explored them all. In the afternoons, my boss came and sat at the edge of my desk, like a hip teacher, and tried on being a thoughtful man. He was always trying to sell me things that were allegedly good for me – almond butter, aloe vera juice, himself. His face was stupidly handsome and so symmetrical it made me roll my eyes to the ceiling. He wasn't perfect though. I noticed he had a hidden aggressive streak and, at times, I suspected he was responsible for the absent bin men. Also, he was not someone I went to for love and affection and he was maybe better dressed than I would have liked. I had a lot of problems with him. He was obsessed with success. I felt I was under constant inspection, and he had a way of looking me up and down like I was a CV full of errors and misspellings. He was older, but it was hard to pin down anything precise. We went to a lot of dimly lit restaurants. Anytime I thought I got a handle on his age, he ordered another bottle of wine and it was gone again. We talked mostly about the office, the flies that we couldn't get rid of, the people we disliked, how we physically had to wrench ourselves out of bed in the morning. Afterwards we would go back to his and he would attempt one of his two-and-a-half moves. He always fell asleep with both hands on my shoulders like we were in a conga line at a party. *Conga, conga, conga.* Honestly, I hated him.

At first, I worried about it a lot. The worrying made my food come up and up. I came to resemble my father in the early days of his illness; I was surprised when I caught sight of my concentration-camp legs. 'How do they support me?' I wondered. I had no idea but I got high and giddy on the engineering of it. At lunchtime, I ate outside with Paula. The smell of the office forced us into the cold and we sat together shivering over our lunchboxes. Paula's lunch was made up by her husband and always contained the correct amount of protein and carbohydrates. I can't describe the empty, whooshing feeling that went through me when I saw those food combinations. When I found the courage, I asked Paula if, at any stage of her life, she felt herself moving closer to the ground? If the chewing-gum stains on the street were any clearer to her than they used to be?

'I think I'm becoming a hunchback,' I confessed.

Paula was adamant that I was not a hunchback, that my fundamental problem was that I used people to feel attractive. Paula wasn't interested in turning heads. She didn't want men to look at her. Anytime a man looked at her she just picked up the phone and called the refuse collection. I think she was in love with the person on the other end of the line. Their conversations tended to be about Art and Beauty and not about bins at all. In a short space of time, Paula became quite a dangerous woman to know. Slowly, I moved my desk three inches away from hers.

At the weekends, I compensated by overeating. I went to nice places and flirted with the waiters. I bought books on pressure points from charity shops, some of which were highly complex pop-ups. I read these books or I rested them, two at a time, on my head and walked the length of my father's house. As soon as I moved in I realised this house was a mistake. It was too big for me and the stuff I owned shrank by comparison. It looked like I had a wardrobe of baby clothes in those giant, oak cupboards. If I couldn't sleep in one room I just moved to another. It wasn't as suffocating as I needed it to be. Sometimes, I just sat in a tiny space on the sitting-room floor and ran my fingers over those fake 3D backs. It was like seeing a photo of myself with every flaw removed. Often, I played with my father's collectibles. It wasn't a large collection, just two ceramic children, a boy playing the flute, a girl smiling encouragingly, and a shell in which you could hear the sea. I moved the children around the mantelpiece and marvelled at their serenity. I turned them to face outwards; I turned them to face inwards. There wasn't much else to do. I listened to the seashell like it was my last hope.

My boss described the house as 'weird'. He said the whole set-up was 'weird.' Except me. I was cute and he liked to tickle me under the chin, and then take off his clothes. He guessed something was wrong with me lately: in the way I sipped my wines, the way I sat upright and desperately still. He raised the question of me making myself sick.

'Only during the week,' I said, cheerfully, touched by his concern.

We were giving up. Previously, he had listed out my faults with amazing conviction and I truly thought that brought us closer together as a couple. I had no discernible direction in life, I didn't want anything, I was stupid and entitled. Suddenly, he acted as if he didn't care whether I knew these things or not. Instead, he said, 'Okay I'm going to make myself come now,'—as if removing me from the whole act was a sort of kindness. All that was left to talk about was what we'd do to the bin men if we ever found them. Our last night together I folded up my blouse and asked him to perform a thermal massage on my back and growing hump. He refused. Several weeks later, he called me into his office. There had been complaints from anonymous staff. I was never at my desk. He said it was imperative an assistant be at his or her desk.

'Where exactly are you?'

At home I was learning how to self-massage and was feeling pretty fulfilled. I had no interest in my job anymore but I tried. My concentrating face required more effort than genuine concentration. The organisation of the face, the setting up of the features, was exhausting. Afterwards, I often lay down on the cold tiles of the office bathroom floor and didn't move for hours. On normal days I did my job correctly, I counted and pointed and made pleasant popping noises with my mouth, but now there were no normal days. My boss suggested time off. To grieve.

He said I was a brilliant assistant but my father's death had affected me deeply. Take a holiday, he said. I muttered something about the restorative properties of the sea and went home to my sitting-room with its battered, springless couch. Before I left, Paula gave me one of those insincere half hugs. I smiled, thinking of the polite phrasing of the email that was probably sent around informing everyone of my departure.

Without work, I had hours and hours to fill. I performed difficult bending exercises. There was a futility and pointlessness to the whole procedure that I found particularly moving. These exercises had a sighing soundtrack I provided. I skimmed over articles on graceful posture: Pretend to be brimming with self-confidence. Pretend to be a movie star. Pretend to be a human being. At night, I tried to forget about it. I stayed out, alone. On the way home, drunk, I took bits of songs I heard in taxis and applied them to my own life. For the first time ever, I was meeting people. Full of my own brazen ugliness, I was just walking out into the night and finding them.

I considered myself pretty tolerant of people and open to new experiences and ideas. I didn't often seek out experiences but when they were presented to me I usually liked them. I took the new people out to meet college friends, beautiful sad girls who dressed like widows and claimed the world had crushed them, cruelly, like 'matchboxes'. Most of the new people were shy in their company. The men, usually men, often older, never joined in. They just looked at me like that was what they were supposed to do. It was unnerving. They smelled like crackers, sometimes crackers and cheese, sometimes crackers and another substance, but there was always a distinctive cracker smell in the air. My friends had their jackets on before they finished their drinks. I felt I was being thought of as 'inappropriate' and, in response, dug out dry skin from my scalp and discarded it on the floor beneath me. The men sat still and silent as dummies.

'What do you want from all this?' the girls asked. I didn't know. I was never a big dreamer. Maybe someone to wave at who feebly waves back? These women thought of me as typical: not tragic enough, but still capable of pulling stunts that lowered the calibre of their beauty. I counted the number of times I had touched them all, appraised their imperfections, cheered at their hickeys and sex bruises. It occurred to me that I could never ask any of these women to pour aromatherapy oils over my back, gently and without judgement. They would never rub their hands along my spine and check for signs of roundness whilst making soft reassurances. They were there for me in the ways they should be, at the funeral they formed a neat cluster and discreetly cried, but that was where it stopped. I wanted them to say: 'Thank you, thank you so much for everything you have done for us and our self-esteem.' I wanted them to cheer the fuck up. They didn't cheer up though and they didn't express gratitude. They just wafted out of the building and I straightened my back at them. The men continued to stare at me like I was an item of significant interest.

I needed these friendships to go somewhere. I made certain alterations to my lifestyle for these old men. I dusted, I tidied away my father's collection, I cleaned out my bathroom cabinet so it resembled the cabinet of a woman who had very little to worry about. I saw myself making these slight adjustments. I watched as if it was an instructive montage about how a person can take purposeful strides in their life. The music that accompanied these scenes was sassy and upbeat. I suddenly gave a shit and it suited me.

My father used to ask if I cared about other people at all and the correct answer was 'Yes'. I did. I cared, I cared, I cared. I had healthy friendships in mind. Things should have been easier when I got the men alone but they never were. I wanted them to talk, to tell me everything, about their families, and the minor incidents that destroyed them, and maybe the moments they had ruined by doing or saying the wrong thing. What then? What then? But, nothing. Their eyes just roamed around like they were searching for something better beyond my head. Of course, they were all seized by a singular fear when I began my striptease. I guess it was because I was always more involved in the tease than the strip. I liked jokes, death jokes, single-girl jokes, and was shocked when these didn't lead naturally to a friendly situation.

Sometimes, when the fingers were flying over the front of my blouse, I thought: 'This is hilarious. No, actually, this is an illness. This inability to take anything seriously. I should get money from the state.' Afterwards, I compensated by lying. I'd been let go, I'd been promoted, I do this, I do that, who cares? In a second of stupidity and weakness, I told one of them about my developing hump. I may have curled up on his chest and cried. I may have beaten his chest lightly with my fists. He promised that if we stayed together he would love me all the same. He wasn't begging but he nearly was. After he left the house, in the half-dark, I caught him on the street, kicking a taxi. It was an embarrassing situation.

The time came to return to work but I couldn't do it. It wasn't so much the job as the confusion and frustration that went with it. Standing and sitting and breathing in the stale air of people who despised me – I couldn't face it. I rang up HR and told them my boss made a pass at me. I said I hoped it accounted for some of my odder behaviour in the few weeks before my departure.

HR asked: 'What happened?'
I said: 'Well, he brought me into his office.'
HR said: 'Of course, he did. He's your boss.'
I said: 'He sat across from me at the table.'
HR said nothing.

I said: 'He leaned quite far across the table.'
HR said nothing.
I said: 'It was a very small table.'

I was granted a further two weeks holiday, fully paid. I decided to use that money to invest in my future. I visited various chemists and I had a lot of questions. 'Is it more politically correct to say: I have a hump or I am a hunchback?' The counter girls made funny clicking noises with their teeth and I pined for my own lost work noises. They prescribed yoga classes that promised to straighten my spine and make me wholesome at the same time. Things were too trippy for me in that tiny room and I found all the goodness smothering. Anything could happen in that blissed-out state and that seemed idiotic and negligent so I stopped going.

A backscratcher appeared in my room, leftover from a previous life when back-scratching was something to look forward to. I slept beside it, and at night, it extended its long-armed sympathies towards me. When I woke up beside that disembodied hand, I didn't feel so bad. I went to a general store which felt illegal and like I was breaking a code – my friends and I were fonder of expensive, specific things. In the queue, fly-swatter in hand, I asked myself if I looked like a sophisticated person. I didn't. I closed my eyes and imagined hitting the hump downwards with tools and quiet prayers. In the lamplight of my luckless bedroom, I delivered fast, brisk strokes to the centre of my back. I found it hard to keep a straight face.

I saw a chiropractor. I made that choice. A solid man who searched his hands up and down my back as if looking for someone to blame. He was tall and boring and told me he went canoeing at weekends. I asked, 'How many tall men can you fit in a canoe?' which sounded like the beginning of something, a riff or an innuendo, but was a real and genuine query. The gap in my canoe knowledge was huge and overwhelming. I told him I imagined my hump would be a large square shape, like a heavy schoolbag full of difficult homework. He frowned and flipped me over. He didn't look like a chiropractor at all. He looked like a hippie, or a child's lazy drawing of a hippie. All he could offer was drugs and hand-holding, neither of which I wanted. Before I left, he gave me a tissue and said, 'In case you get upset.' I would never get upset in that sort of room with that sort of man, but I stuck the tissue in my sleeve for safe-keeping. After that, there was nothing, just wide-open spaces, like the reception desk and the world. On the way out, I passed a girl with a neat bob and thought: That's me. I could be that girl. I could be a girl with a bob. She asked if I needed to make another appointment. I told her to schedule me in every month for the foreseeable future and to adopt an air of discretion when she greeted me at the desk. I did not expect to be treated vastly differently, I was a standard hunchback, but a smile or kind word might ease a burden. The bob put her hand over her mouth like a silent-movie actress. Where do they even find these women? She steadied herself on her chair as I shuffled away.

My life, and what I did with it, became a sort of mystery then. I reorganised my father's collection, I called Paula and heard the phone ring out and out, I took an aversion to the shower tray. I removed traces of my father from his own home. I needed it so that he wasn't my father, that I didn't know him, that I had never even heard of him. I wrote my boss a letter. It was titled: 'I'm Sorry'. Prompted by this letter he rang me and said he was sorry too and let's meet, let's be two sorry people in the same room. I dressed up for it. I took my time. I wanted him to wait and I wanted to be the thing he was waiting for.

In the lobby of the cinema he was nothing like I remembered; angrier, shorter. He looked like a small town I might live in and die. He told me there had been a confrontation with the bin men and he had been fired. His arm was in a cast. During the film, anytime he turned towards me, the cast rubbed off my face. Afterwards, we stood on the street and I thought he was going to kiss me or grab me or do something obvious. Instead, he pulled my hand and placed two of my fingers on his bare neck. 'Can you feel that lump? Right there?' I rubbed a small swollen mark from where the shirt of his collar had been closed too tightly. 'That's cancer, I think. It's cancer more than likely.' I agreed that it probably was cancer, that he had caught it early. He asked me if I wanted a drink and I said no, thank you. It was important to me that I was polite.

When I left him, I felt a happy relief. I thought of night classes, the sea, re-decorating.

Abortion, a Love Story

Some names and places have been changed. This text went to press before the end of rehearsals and so may differ slightly from the play performed.

NATASHA

When Natasha walked into Professor Carr's office, she was embarrassed. Her embarrassment didn't stem from her own absences and tragic results, the reason why she was there, but from the walls and walls of books that imprisoned the professor. A middle-aged man – whose questions in his seminars prompted no answers, and who secretly felt his deep knowledge of his subjects was hindering him in a world becoming superficial – he laid out his plump, hairy hands on the desk in front of Natasha.

Natasha knew this was a man who had spent a long time establishing a reputation, and now he had a reputation and nothing else. She felt deep, incommunicable pity for him.

'I have a disorder,' she said, pre-empting him. 'I can't explain exactly what my disorder is but it prevents me from absorbing any knowledge into my brain.'

Natasha thought about her disorder a lot – how it had developed, how it was particularly alert to moments of boredom. She wasn't even fully sure how she ended up in the college, which was separated from the outside world by large and forbidding gates, an oasis in an uncaring city. She remembered reading through the college brochures and picking the place with the oldest, leafiest trees, the highest buildings. This was where she would get most value for money, she decided. As for classes, she attended one here and there, but, now she was in final year, she realised you were supposed to go to many classes, one after another. Education was sequential and the building blocks had to be laid.

She no longer knew what she was studying. Out of panic and blind fear, and an increasing pounding in her chest, she had taken to stuffing her ears with cotton wool so she couldn't hear a single word in the gated community. It was the start of January and she spent most of her time sitting, completely still, in Front Square. She quivered with anger on the stone bench. Lately, her anger was an uncontrollable thing: it trailed her everywhere, making her ugly.

'Natasha, your results aren't up to scratch. If you don't do something now you probably won't graduate.'

'The unemployment building,' Natasha said, with finality.

The unemployment building hung like a threat over the final year student body. They had heard various things: that it was a place where men smoked openly and hacked into their elbows; where paint peeled from the walls as if trying to escape; where their immune systems would be lowered and threatened by ancient illnesses. Many of the students were leaving for the outside world with confidence, heading for financial institutions, their family businesses. Whenever Natasha was sighted, the other students admired her careless style and seeming disregard for everything, but she was clearly marked. If anyone mentioned the unemployment building to her in passing, she simply said, 'At least it's honest. I find the college experience corrupt.' Like a president under threat of assassination, she refused to show fear in public.

'I know what fourth year feels like, Natasha,' Professor Carr said. 'It feels like the end of a party.'

'I've never been to a party.' She gazed out the window. The city was moving closer, the buildings pressing in on her. 'I have a lot of self-control,' she said, by way of explanation.

'Okay. Well, let's see if we can do anything about these grades.'

She continued staring out the window. 'I can't be saved.'

'Where do you think your problems began?'

She thought. 'The computer house.'

The computer house was a glass building attached to the library and, in the last year, it had become a symbol to Natasha of the college regime. The structure was a mystery to her. Most days, out of curiosity, she ventured up and peered inside at the productive people busying themselves around the printing station. Often she imagined herself walking into the computer house, opening a document, putting words on that document, deliberate, incisive words about the subject she was studying. Then, standing at the printing station, with complete attentiveness, waiting for her document. With the best of intentions, she stood outside and thought about going inside. Usually, she was running away before she even noticed she was running away. Her fear wasn't fully irrational. The last time she had been inside, in late November, she had received an email from an account she didn't recognise, describing scenes from her life. They were written like the darkest play – her uninspiring daily routine, her arguments with her boyfriend, one scene delivered in unfathomable poetic language – all ripped directly from her life. She hadn't checked her emails since.

'I don't think the computer house has done anything to you, Natasha.'

'I think I'm being watched.'

Professor Carr leaned forward on the desk, as if preparing to deliver a sermon. 'Every woman in this country is being watched.'

'But I specifically feel like I'm being watched.'

They sat in silence.

'I hear the unemployment building is a lot like hell,' Natasha said, after a while.

'You should be grateful that you're young.'

'I want youth to be over. I don't like it.' She thought of the hours she spent on the stone bench waiting for youth to pass. She often sat for so long, morning to evening, that she heard the six o'clock bell signalling religion. She knew time moved strangely inside the gated community. She was largely indifferent to her fellow students with their loud typing on computers, and the ideas they communicated to each other in trembling voices. They all seemed to follow a strict code and, in the college coffee shop, they outlined their secret philosophies passionately, huddled beneath heavy cardigans. 'What are you all talking about?' Natasha wanted to scream. Ideas, ideas, ideas. She had no time for ideas. She wasn't raised with ideas.

'I don't like it,' Natasha repeated.

'Natasha, we only have a few months. Let me help you.'

'But my disorder,' she said, weakly.

When Professor Carr discovered what a philistine Natasha actually was, he dedicated himself to her general cultural education. He instructed her to come up to his office three times a week. As he listed out books to her, Natasha counted the hairs on the backs of his hands. There were six longer hairs and three shorter ones. Had she read the Americans – Bellow, Roth, Auster? How was her philosophy – Toussaint, Nietzsche, Baudrillard? Had she seen *That Obscure Object of Desire*? Had she seen *Vertigo*?

He screened films for her as she lay on the carpeted floor of his office. She positioned her body so he could see down her top. She felt as if she were slowly seducing a priest through a confessional grille. She watched the lint from the carpet rise and fall. Soft carpet was still new to her.

'Do you understand it's about the danger of possession and the futility of desire?' he asked.

She looked at him sadly. 'All the money he spent on that suit. What a waste.'

Natasha felt altruistic during these trips, like she was throwing pieces of bread to a starving duck. The professor acted innocent, like nothing had happened with a student before, but Natasha wasn't sure. She felt like he might have gotten away with a lot in his office simply because of the size and shape of it. Despite her doubts, when she first touched him, on her sixth appearance, she giggled – playing the virgin – and he blushed right down to the back of his hands.

*

When Natasha first entered college, at eighteen, a boy called Patrick, stick-thin, raised Catholic, had attached himself to her. He was her first boyfriend. They were a good pairing because she was a strange person pretending to be a normal person, and he was a normal, well-raised person desperately pretending to be strange. She knew when they left college he would get a job in a bank, develop financial ideas. He was the sole link to a life Natasha felt she could never fully be part of. Already she suspected love was over for her. How could you make another person happy? How could they make you happy?

During the day, she wandered the campus with Patrick – avoiding her classes, the buildings looming over them, the city, outside the walls, doing whatever it did in its daylight hours – and he filled her in on the comings and goings of the place. She worried, despite all preventative measures being taken, self-control barriers being right-fully installed, her daily exercise regime producing slick, metallic sweat, that she had inherited her mother's weak and crazy personality. Her mind felt like a long trailer carrying a number of cars; if one car went they would all go, scatter across the motorway, cause carnage. She would miss her sanity when it went.

She wanted to spend her weekends like the other students, underground, undernourished, blacking out, being infinitely surprised by her own youth and beauty, but she didn't allow herself. In her entire college career, she hadn't had one bit of fun and was immensely proud of this fact. Fun was forbidden to her. She might enjoy it too much and slip into the endless pursuit of it. At least she was charming, she assured herself. But charm was thin compensation for a life of constant, lurking terror.

Her relationship with Patrick had become queasier and queasier. In September she had fallen pregnant and she'd asked him to steal money from his parents to pay for the abortion.

'Steal money from *your* father,' he said. 'I'm not a thief.'

'Why are you this way, Patrick?' she asked, in genuine bafflement.

The night before she travelled, Patrick, counting out the cash, looked like he might cry. 'It's okay if you want to cry,' he said to Natasha.

'I don't,' she replied. 'I'm not sure if you know this but I had a very tough childhood and have had to overcome obstacles far greater than this to seal my place in the elite college.'

'You don't go to any of your classes.'

'I have a disorder,' she said. 'Anyway you're only upset because you think you're supposed to be. You don't care about me.'

He didn't correct her. It was as if he couldn't procure an abortion and lie in the same week. It would have to be one or the other. In the clinic she sat in the waiting room, trying to figure out how she was supposed to feel, wondering who to blame, nurturing her anger. It all happened in a flash. Although she was alone, she didn't feel alone, she felt like a part of a large pantomime dragon made up of other women, a long line of them, moving and swaying invisibly through the city. When she returned, she and Patrick stayed together. It was around then she stopped attending college full-time and starting using the cotton wool more liberally.

At the weekends, when Patrick went out to clubs, she stayed in his family home and cooked him hearty lasagnes. She bought a special apron. She wanted to look proper, like a girl who would never steal, never have an abortion. The apron was a plastic material; every stain wiped right off. She bought it in the luxury department store. On Saturday nights she watched television in the good living room with his parents, who loved her like an orphan.

Patrick arrived home on the edge of Sunday evenings, looking strange, dirty, with that shame he carried in his shoulders whenever he had been cheating on her. Whoever he had been sleeping with, Natasha still got an almighty thrill watching him eat those lasagnes. As she layered the ingredients the red of the mince reminded her of her father's bloody mouth, huge and open, at their kitchen table. To calm herself, she often locked herself in the bathroom and counted the perfumes, emerging extremely fragrant. She didn't eat any of the lasagnes and if Patrick started telling her about the fun he had at the clubs – what a glorious good time it all was – she just stood up and left the room. Afterwards, they had sex tentatively, lightly, as if neither of them wanted to be involved any more. On one of their last weekends together, Patrick, a psychology student, said that God had appeared to him in a dream and told him the only real addiction Natasha had inherited from her mother was her addiction to pain.

'Maybe God should have diagnosed me before you got me pregnant,' she said.

Finally, in the college coffee shop, their relationship was coming to a close. She slid a cold lasagne across the table as a symbol of their time together.

'I don't like you anymore,' she announced.

'You don't like anything, Natasha.'

It was true. One day, as a challenge, she set herself the task of writing down everything she didn't like. She filled an entire copybook with her tiny, hateful handwriting. She included the elite college at least forty-five times. She included the concept of fun ten times. She included Patrick eighteen times.

She shrugged. 'Goodbye, Patrick.'

Patrick tapped his fingers meditatively across his nose, subsuming this rejection into his grand, personal narrative within a few short seconds, and stood up. He didn't say goodbye. When he was safely out of sight, Natasha took out the ornate cigarette case in which she kept her cotton wool. She had to be careful she didn't hear any opinions in the coffee shop. She crammed some in her ears and began to cry. Normally, she didn't understand her fellow students' need for melancholy, their high emotional register, shrieking music and complete lack of composure like they were auditioning daily for some drama she wanted nothing to do with. She had to keep her emotions quiet and fixed in place or her whole face would break apart. But this was the end of her first romance and she was determined to enjoy it. She wept loudly, not knowing herself if they were fake or real tears; she attracted a lot of attention from nearby tables. Her father's false teeth appeared to her that night, their cold porcelain chattering in the silver of her dreams. For once she could hear what they said: 'Natasha, don't lose your mind.'

*

Natasha's days passed as a series of empty diary dates, no classes attended and no closer to discovering what she was studying. Inside the campus, the students stripped themselves of their wool jumpers and cardigans, and lay awake at night worrying about their results. Natasha didn't lie awake at night. She slept heavily and had wild dreams where she was watched by a thousand eyes, chased down corridors. It felt absurd to continue her service in the college.

She was now involved with the professor after a protracted and fraught seduction he had feebly protested. Overall, they didn't have much to say to each other; they didn't speak the same language on account of the significant age gap, but it didn't matter. As they hid in hallways, lay secretly on the carpet in his office, Natasha felt like she was involved in a transaction that was professional and centuries old. It was a history lesson. While Professor Carr tried to educate her she adopted an expression of complete neutrality.

'Of course, you've heard of Ionesco.'

'You should have seen where I grew up. I was like the roadrunner in that awful cartoon, constantly evading a terrible fate.'

'It can't have been that bad, Natasha.'

'You have no idea.'

When they ventured out together, into the city's understanding night, to its high-priced bars and restaurants, she couldn't help but think of the city's own romantic past – all the liaisons it had hosted without its consent. Going out in the city was exciting for Natasha; she had to be stern with herself, and be extra careful not to have any fun.

'Do you think other people are having liaisons in the city right now?' she asked.

They were in a taxi, sitting far apart.

'I suppose.'

'Do you think two people having a liaison ever sat in this exact same taxi?'

'Probably.'

'The circle of life,' Natasha said, dreamily.

He agreed but Natasha could see tears forming in the corners of his eyes. Since he met Natasha he was prone to excessive weeping. He wept whenever she mentioned anything contemporary. He wept when she told him she hadn't accumulated any significant life regrets. He wept when she admitted to some laziness in her academic work. The real issue was Natasha made him feel like a young man and he hadn't liked being a young man. She enraged him and brought him back to a time when all women were inscrutable. One night he confronted her with her blank academic diary. She watched him waving it in front of her, like evidence of an indiscretion.

'Who are *you*?' he asked. 'Why do you have so few time commitments?'

The next day, to appease him, and with a hope of finding out what she was studying, she visited the computer house. It was as bad as she remembered, full of irritating, flickering computers.

There were several emails from her father. He sent her articles about the importance of the college, what it had achieved, dead facts and figures. He also sent her clips from TV sketch shows they had watched together. After her mother left, they had watched comedies, takeaways resting on their laps. Splayed over couches in that sitting-room – their eyes glued on the television set, laughing over the same stupid scenes, sticky food dropping onto the stiff carpet – they had buried her mother, although, somewhere, she was still alive.

If she and her father wanted to express anything, they did it in the ugly, hideous, hilarious language of the shows. He attached a clip of a man screaming down a telephone about a hotel reservation, with the sentence: 'Natasha, this is funny!' Natasha wrote back: 'They don't like that stuff here,' because she wanted to tell the truth and also she wanted to hurt him which was, occasionally, the same thing.

As she scrolled through the emails, on the whirring machine next to hers, a small, first year girl moved through photos of another young girl. Through the fast succession of images, Natasha watched as the onscreen girl stood and knelt in different poses. Close-up. Her make-up was slick and robotic, adhering to regulations. Larger view. Full-length shot. Two thumbs hooked under the strings of her vest. Nipples flared towards the camera.

'Who's that person?' Natasha asked, tapping the monitor.

The first year girl focused on her screen as if willing Natasha to disappear. She ran her tongue over her parched lips. 'Nobody,' she said, after some consideration. She carefully angled her whole body away.

The last email Natasha opened was a single stage direction: *The girl sits alone, waiting, in the clinic.*

After much aggravated typing, she located an academic email. She searched for evidence of what she was studying as the hazy sunlight shone on the computer house. She couldn't organise the words into sentences, she couldn't read the words, she felt hatred towards the words. All of this transpired within a few short seconds. The hazy light shone on.

*

One night, two months into their rather tedious liaison, while seated in a mid-priced restaurant, the professor told Natasha she reminded him of the music of his era – which he had loved *at the time*, which he had needed to feel alive *at the time* – but now whenever he listened back, with intelligence and reason, it was baffling. It was just a lot of empty noise. When he heard that music now, jagged and alienating, he felt one foul swoop of nostalgia before he realised it was all rather silly. He had no idea how he had ever danced to it.

'You probably just did this,' she raised her hands in the air and swayed gently.

'Please put your hands down.'

This was their love. Sadly unrhythmic. Silly.

'You're not like the others,' the professor said, doubtfully.

'What others?'

Afterwards when they went back to his bachelor apartment, Natasha wanted to watch trash TV. The professor owned a large plasma screen that was perfectly suited to trash viewing. Her incredible self-control didn't naturally extend to her taste in television. She tried to frame it critically, but it was straight-up, stick-in-your-teeth trash. Natasha had romance visions like anyone her age. She wasn't a girl who doodled in her notebook and never had been, but she entertained scenarios. In her fantasies, they watched *Breast Implants Gone Wrong* with feeling and sincerity. Firstly, they would marvel at how fine and normal the breasts were before they underwent any surgical procedures. As they watched the horror unfold, Natasha would cry knowledgeably over what women do to their bodies. Then she would swan around the room, naked, her unremarkable breasts framed in a newly appreciated light.

She didn't get this opportunity. Instead they watched a film where time was the enemy and ageing was a singular tragedy: a film about a middle-aged man. Natasha lay face down, her head buried in the bedsheets, her hands locked over her ears, while the film was happening. She had an instinct for self-preservation and she knew if she caught sight of a single scene, even for a second, it would reduce her life span by several years. She understood the professor was watching the film, thinking wistfully of his lost youth, and Natasha's failings as a student, of which there were several hundred, and her failings as a human being, of which there were also several hundred. As the film neared its climax, he placed the thinner of the two bedsheets over his head and cried, taking in huge gulps of air like an inconsolable ghost.

'I know you're crying under there,' she said.

The sheet sniffled.

'Did I ever tell you that when my mother left my father he pulled out his front two teeth with a pliers? I didn't understand it then but I'm starting to now. Love is very hard.'

'What was your mother like?'

'She was like me.'

The sheet nodded.

*

As they reached the three-month mark, that milestone creeping up on them both, draining them of all life and hope, the professor's expression became more resigned, his great height reduced to a stoop, his suits creased and untidy as if he were choosing to get dressed in the dark to avoid his reflection. In the evenings, when he walked towards Natasha, down the more secretive ramps, it wasn't the walk of a man who has won the sexual jackpot. It was the frozen gait of someone who wanted to ask: 'Is this still happening to me? Is it?'

At dinner, that night, squashed into a small corner booth, in a low-priced restaurant, he looked around, frantically, as if pleading for someone to help him. Natasha could see the other diners thinking – that lucky soul. But mostly they could only see the back of his head. Natasha could see the whole thing and it wasn't a pretty picture. Only the most macabre and disturbed of painters would enjoy creating a scene like this. The front of him, especially his gentle ageing face, was stricken. He was acutely aware that he had made a mistake and his mistake was sitting opposite him, munching cheerfully on vegetables.

'Eat up,' Natasha shoved his plate towards him. 'Enjoy yourself. We're having a liaison.'

She could be mildly badgering, mildly abusive. It was a result of her control problems. The professor looked like he might cry again.

'Let me tell you about my childhood.'

'Natasha, please,' the professor said, putting down his fork. 'You have to rise above your circumstances.'

'I'm not a character in one of your films. It's not that easy.'

'You must try.'

'What if I don't want to?'

'Don't get sentimental about the place you grew up,' he said. 'That's for pedestrian minds.'

'Excuse me,' Natasha said and stood up angrily. She walked to the bathroom. In the mirror she watched her face. She felt bilocated. She wasn't here, but she wasn't there either. She looked at her reflection like they were in on the same joke. In the cubicle, she shredded some tissue, threw it in the air and watched it fall like wedding confetti. She knew someone would have to clean that up. She had no excuses for why she did the things she did. She was sick of the cleanliness of the college, the neat angles, the smooth walls of the buildings, the gates that slammed shut. She saw the professor's pristine bedroom as an extension of the college. She was sick of reason and order; she wanted filth and chaos. She thought of the dim basement bar her mother used to bring her to as a child, and how the college was the same really – no better, no more worthy. Everybody with their own solitary pains, their own endless private afflictions, but nobody looking anybody directly in the eye and asking what they were. Let's turn up the music and pretend we're having a hell of a time in here. She looked in the mirror again. Her face was just a sack of skin. Her face was totally white, and she considered the possibility that, after a long wait, she was finally falling apart.

When she walked back through the restaurant, skirting around tables, she heard the professor laughing loudly. As she got closer to the booth, she realised there was another girl sitting in her place. She was maybe twenty, her hair was messy and she was wearing a dirty green coat with gold buttons. Underneath her coat Natasha could see a short dress, tight and tacky. Her eye make-up was black, heavily and expertly applied in thick streams. She looked like what was promised to men when they returned from war. She looked like a deep, dark forbidden river. She was also, from all appearances, monstrously drunk.

'Welcome to the good life!' the girl shouted.

'You're in my seat,' Natasha said.

'Natasha,' Professor Carr said, 'this is Lucy.'

'Hi.' Lucy extended her hand.

Natasha stamped to the other side of the booth. She slid in beside Professor Carr. She smoothed down her floral-print dress. To calm herself, she thought of all the beautiful things she had ever worn in her life.

'I don't like anybody my own age,' she said, after a while.

'What's wrong with you?' Lucy asked. 'Did you have an argument with your boyfriend?'

'He's not my boyfriend. We're having a liaison.'

'How nice.'

'I've just met Lucy,' Professor Carr said.

'It's marvellous,' Lucy added, smiling.

Natasha was silent.

To ease the tension, Professor Carr signalled for the waiter. Lucy held the menu for a long time, shaking in excitement. 'I like to order a lot of food,' she said, 'and then eat all of it.' She dragged her finger through the menu, marking things off to the waiter. She ordered two starters, two mains and two desserts. 'I like food that is lumpy and improper,' she announced to the table. She insisted on three bottles of a bubbly drink that was close to champagne. 'This is all I drink now. Bring everything together.' Natasha watched this display in fascination as Professor Carr rested his hands on both their knees.

'You're a pig,' Natasha said.

'Do you like to have fun, Natasha?'

'It's a waste of time.'

'I like it. I like parties.'

'So do I,' Professor Carr said. He struck Natasha in that moment, despite his education, as a fool. He was the most foolish she had ever seen him.

'If you want,' Lucy said, 'you can compliment me until the food arrives.'

'I will start,' Professor Carr said.

'Don't compliment me,' Natasha said. 'Don't dare compliment me. I will vomit all over this table if you even pass one single compliment in my direction.'

'Natasha has a lot of anger,' Professor Carr said.

Lucy turned to Natasha. 'How long have you had anger?'

'A year. Maybe more than a year.'

'It doesn't suit most people,' Lucy said, 'but I think it suits you. You bear it well.'

'Thank you.'

When the food and drink arrived, Lucy spread out the plates and arranged them as if there were a particular system, a definite hierarchy, but she ate everything in different orders, regardless. She dipped chips into reservoirs of ketchup and danced them in the air, as she held her almost-champagne flute in her other hand. She let chocolate ice cream dribble down her chin. She drank at a reckless speed. She drank like she was trying to quench a fire, except that fire was heavily dispersed and within herself. Professor Carr giggled, a high-pitched shriek that drove Natasha to the brink of her sanity; and he pushed his hands further up their legs. With her mouth full, Lucy spoke about the holiday she had been on recently and how it had changed her immeasurably. Had either of them been to the edge of the world to discover them-selves? Had they lain on an uncomfortable mattress and watched the sun rise and fall like it was string-operated? Travel was now fundamental to her human make-up. But she was only in second year and was stranded on the island of college for another two years.

'I believe I've been sent to this college as a punish-ment for something I did in a past life,' she said, as she gnawed at a piece of chicken. 'That's the only way to explain it.'

Natasha had the same fear, but she didn't voice it.

Lucy uncorked another bottle and continued. She found a lot about the college disgusting but what she found most disgusting was how all the girls from the country came up, got rich city boyfriends, as if it finally saved them and, of course, they stayed in the boy's family home all weekend, being so impressed by the house, eating their expensive cheeses or whatever. It was boring, right? She wouldn't do it. And these guys made such a production of introducing you to their parents. Who cares? Everyone has parents.

'Do you have parents?' Natasha asked.

Lucy looked directly at her. 'No.'

'Where in the countryside are you from? Your accent is familiar.'

'I don't know,' Lucy said, 'I can't remember.'

She carried on as if there had been no interruption. What was most boring was how all these guys would leave college, develop certain financial ideas, marry women from their wealthy villages, buy them cars to shut them up when they had affairs. And the worst thing was they accused her of being shallow. Once you saw underneath, once the curtain had been lifted, the show was over. The place was a farce. How were you supposed to take it seriously at all? She hiccuped and began breathing into her glass.

'Lucy,' Professor Carr said, cheerfully, 'is a writer.'

'No, she's not.'

'She is. She reminds me a lot of a young Sontag.'

Lucy knocked over her glass. 'That's fine,' she slurred, watching the fizzy liquid spread across the tablecloth. 'Don't worry about that.'

'She's written a play.'

Natasha froze.

'The most important thing about these guys is not to get pregnant from one of them,' Lucy said, 'you just wouldn't trust them, would you? You wouldn't feel comfortable.'

Natasha stared at her.

'What's your play about, Lucy?' Professor Carr asked.

'I was crazy when I wrote that. I was really crazy.'

'And you're not now?' Natasha asked.

'No,' Lucy smiled, 'I'm feeling clear-minded now.'

Professor Carr, giddy, drove his hands still further up their legs.

'What are you going to do when you leave college in a few months, Natasha?' Lucy asked.

'Natasha is going to the unemployment building,' Professor Carr said, with confidence.

Natasha sat up straight. 'I might become an artist.'

'Oh really? And what will you make art about?'

'My childhood.'

'Oh God,' Professor Carr muttered.

'Maybe you could write a play? Do you like the theatre?'

'Not really.'

'Natasha doesn't like anything,' Professor Carr said.

'I thought you might like it because you're studying it.'

There was a long, grateful silence.

'Thank you,' Natasha said.

'You have a reputation for being strange, you know.'

'That,' Natasha said, 'is unproven.'

Lucy smiled at her in a secret way. 'Anyway, I hate this college,' she said. 'I wish they would leave a window open or something so I could wriggle out and escape.'

'Me too,' Natasha said.

'I know from my travels that the world is wilder than they have led us to believe in there.'

'It's a terrible world,' Professor Carr said. 'Terrible.'

'Natasha, do you know he's married?' Lucy asked.

'I am,' Professor Carr said. 'It's a personal thing so I didn't mention it.'

Natasha pictured herself at Professor Carr's funeral, in the back, in head-to-toe black. A harlot. Their relationship was even less pleasant than she thought it was.

'Natasha,' Lucy asked, 'has anyone ever made a speech in your honour?'

'No. I'm considered too ridiculous.'

In one swift motion, Lucy kicked off her shoes and clambered up on the table, knocking over cutlery and several glasses. 'Whoops,' she said. 'There are a lot of knives and forks on this table.' She took a long swig from the nearest bottle. 'Excuse me, excuse me,' she announced to the restaurant, 'I would like to make a speech.'

'Oh good,' Professor Carr said, 'a speech.'

The diners turned to face Lucy. She swung her dirty coat.

'To Natasha,' she said, 'when she first came to this college, she met a religious boy.'

Someone in the restaurant groaned.

'But he was a dud,' Lucy said. 'He wouldn't listen to anybody and when he kissed he did this with his tongue.' Lucy opened her mouth and jerked her tongue furiously.

'It's true. He did,' Natasha added.

'There's no reason on earth to stay with a man like that,' Lucy continued. 'In the beginning I didn't understand Natasha but then I read her emails and I realised she's an irreplaceable person.'

'Excuse me?'

'Are you sure you read the right emails?' Professor Carr asked.

'So put your glasses up for Natasha now. She's had it tough.' She paused. 'Now!'

The diners put down their cutlery and raised their glasses. 'To Natasha,' Lucy said sweetly. 'To Natasha,' the restaurant chorused. Lucy stepped down and climbed back into the booth.

'How do you know everything about me?'

'I'm done,' Lucy said. 'Goodnight lady, goodnight gentleman. Let's do this again sometime.' She threw herself face first onto her plate and began drooling.

Professor Carr and Natasha sat in silence. Their relationship was destroyed beyond repair. Natasha thought about her patience and her self-control, and how all of that was useless to her now.

'Well,' Professor Carr said.

'Is she okay? Does she do this a lot?'

'I only met her for the first time tonight too,' he said. 'I think she's asleep. She has a head full of dreams.'

'Should we help her?'

'She will be fine.'

He squeezed Natasha's arm gently before he stood and went to the bathroom. Natasha surveyed the wreckage around her, the broken glass, the empty bottles, the destruction. She felt like she might have just attended a party? Her first ever party. There was even a girl passed out beside her; a hopeless corpse.

The corpse opened one blue eye. Natasha screamed. 'Is he gone?' Lucy asked.

She lifted her head off the plate and sighed deeply. She seemed suddenly sober. 'Do you think he's going to be talking when he gets back?'

'He might be.'

Lucy took out an ornate cigarette case from her tiny handbag.

'You can't smoke in here.'

Lucy flipped open the case and turned it to face Natasha. It contained three straight rows of cotton wool. 'I put this stuff in my ears,' Lucy explained, 'when I don't want to listen to people.'

Natasha rummaged for her own cigarette case. She opened it. 'So do I,' she whispered.

The two girls smiled and filled their ears. When Professor Carr returned, sat down and began gesticulating and leaning his body against theirs, they couldn't hear him. Lucy took Natasha's hand as his mouth moved in slow motion but no words came out. He let out another high-pitched giggle. Soon, his face became blurrier as the restaurant lights dimmed and flickered until, finally, he disappeared, and only the two girls remained in the booth.

LUCY

Lucy had no idea where she came from. She remembered getting the bus to college and how, as they moved from the countryside to the city, the music on the radio became gentler, more refined. The heat on the bus was oppressive and the material of the seats scratched at the back of her knees. When she disembarked she swore to never get another bus for the rest of her life.

Every two weeks or so, her parents rang from the black hole she sprang from. Their voices were tinny and far away. She didn't know where her money was funnelled from, and had no inclination to find out. The world, in all its bleak and unexplainable misery, was simply not happening. Whenever her new friends asked about growing up in the countryside, she said, 'I had a lot of authentic experiences. Rivers. Trees.'

'Oh,' they murmured collectively but didn't press her on it.

She was studying theatre and that involved rolling around a wooden floor in a leotard. She was a cat, a bridge, a carton of milk. She was the most malleable student and the instructors ran their hands up her spine. She memorised and recited passages with vigour. Cocteau, Artaud, Sartre. She recited these quotes as if they were filled with the utmost meaning, as if they were designed specifically for her. Her mind had little compartments and her education slid in easily. Her past was disappearing, although she still had dreams. The sky over the college was always a paralysing grey. Every day, in the dance studio, she rested her leg on the wooden bar and limbered up. The wooden bar shook slightly. She recited lines to calm herself. Every week, she shoplifted from the luxury department store.

The first time she walked into the luxury department store, she felt like she was entering a church. The light streamed through the windows; she got to her knees. She had no previous conception that a place like this existed. She had a desire to throw herself out one of the front glass windows because it would be a beautiful, glamorous death. She opened her bag wide and threw in brands. She collected them like quotes – something to show off to her friends. After she shoplifted items she made a careful note of each one in her notebook. She called this notebook, 'Possessions.' She wanted to shoplift from every major brand before she died.

'Is that a political statement?' a drama girl asked when she confessed her ambition.

'Yeah,' Lucy said. 'It's against capitalism.'

In truth, she just wanted the stuff. She put it in another compartment in her brain. She felt when she had shoplifted all the major brands, her true project would be complete.

'Brave,' the drama girl said, snapping the strings of her leotard.

She attended all the lectures and seminars, read the correct books starring shifty Irish male heroes, saw films with shifty French male heroes, squinted at the subtitles, shoplifted the plainest cardigans. 'Can you read that?' she asked loudly in the viewing room as the subtitles tumbled across the screen. 'I can't read that.' She was performing expertly, she was adorable except once, in a seminar, when she shouted, 'Jesus Christ, let me out of here.'

'Who said that, Lucy?' her tutor asked.

'Beckett.'

She couldn't risk a slip-up like that again so she began stuffing her ears with cotton wool, making it easier to agree with people by not listening to them. Her parents' money couldn't keep pace with her life-style. The styles of the cardigans kept changing, wool spooling and unspooling itself across the sky. She slammed her digits into cold machinery. There was nothing that could be done. She didn't speak to her parents anymore; she couldn't even remember their number. Her only memory was them eating plain sandwiches off their laps, and she wasn't even sure that was a real memory or some idea of poverty planted by the college.

'Where does your money come from?' she asked a drama girl.

'I don't know,' the girl said, one leg resting on the wooden bar. 'It just arrives.'

She started sending pictures to men online, her finger in her mouth, her breasts on show, her legs wide open. It was fine. Her accounts filled up. She had one customer called the professor who was particularly fond of her. He claimed that when he looked at her photos, he felt like he was in love, that it had to be love.

'Okay,' Lucy replied and emailed him a list of brands.

'I haven't heard of half of these.'

She drew him a map to the luxury department store.

*

At the start of her second year, Lucy started seeing her first boyfriend, an amateur ventriloquist, majoring in business, who held her hand under tables and called her three times a day to be reassured he was good enough for her. At the weekends, she went out to his family home on the train, speeding past huge houses, glimpsing them sideways. The journey itself felt like an achievement. She bought an apron in the luxury department store to wear around the house. She *bought* it. His parents loved her like an orphan. The apron was a plastic material; every stain wiped right off.

His bedroom was the first place, within those four walls, lying on the soft carpet, she felt safe and her entire ugly history seemed to recede. She was becoming a new person. She fell asleep on top of a pile of stolen cardigans. She read novels and underlined passages that felt special to her in big streaks of red pen. These novels were about civilised women who holidayed in Europe, women whose lives weren't rotten or shameful. Someday, she thought, someday. She would burn her own face off to become one of these women. She still had dreams at night, her boyfriend's arm draped over her; gloomy houses with no exits.

'I'm not good enough for you,' her boyfriend whispered.

'You are,' she insisted.

'I'm not,' he cried and buried his face in the pillow.

She never told him about the pictures, her side-project which she was able to conduct with remarkable distance from herself. She sent picture after picture after picture. Only her body and face were real, the rest was artificial – the lighting, her make-up, her positions. She raised her prices. On every train journey, dressed in increasingly demure cardigans, she found herself falling more in love with her boyfriend. She didn't know what time it was anymore: the digits flew by, clock hands spinning day to night, day to night.

Time moved differently inside the college. She followed the invisible rules closely. No vulgarity. No stupidity. No ugliness. She watched German films, the subtitles even more opaque than the French ones. She was using the cotton wool more and more frequently. On train plat-forms she felt impervious to the weather. She made fairy cakes in her apron, piping the icing carefully.

In his bedroom, looking up at the fake plastic stars affixed to his ceiling, she felt she was no longer a disgust-ing person but an ordinary person, or perhaps even an extraordinary person. Maybe love could transform you in that way. In the photographs, she arched her back like a cat. The glossy finishes looked like layers of plastic.

One night, after a dream about a dark, empty house, she woke up her boyfriend.

'What if I die in college and nobody can identify my body?'

'Lucy,' he said.

'I can't remember what my parents look like.'

'Call them.'

'I don't know their number anymore.'

'Get the bus and go and see them then.'

'I will never get another bus in my life,' she said.

She spent more and more of her time in her boyfriend's family home, abandoning her own tiny room in a student house. Her room was filling relentlessly with *stuff*, gifts from the professor and other customers. Soon the sight of the stuff disgusted her; it dimmed a light in her. She looked up at the plastic stars and told her boyfriend about houses she used to go to as a teenager, stairs she used to walk up, entering rooms made of different air. Nothing normal happened in these rooms.

She told him about how she had to leave her past behind, how she couldn't let it reach her. She had dreams with disagreeable noises. She had dreams with sounds of loud, heavy machinery. She recited lines to keep herself sane. Her boyfriend told her he would protect her, save her. This was love. This was the best the world had to offer.

At night, she wandered her boyfriend's studio, looking at the glassy eyes of the puppets. They were always awake. They never slept. She moved her mouth in time with theirs, as he planned and organised for his debut show. It was a big project, requiring integrity. He had to create a mood. Lucy drifted around the college, eating expensive salads, experiencing the new planet. During the day, she felt so content and serene, so full of love and potential, she thought it might kill her. The college encouraged her to think but she was too busy learning lines to think.

'I haven't done any thinking in three weeks,' she said to her boyfriend. She was looking at the model for the set of his play, the small, vivid world pulled from his imagination. It was bare wooden slats with a light-box to reflect shadows ominously on the walls.

'Thinking is not the thing,' he said, 'artistic impulse is the thing.'

The opening night of his play, in the student theatre, she sat, waiting, in the lobby, peeling an orange. She plopped bits of fruit into her mouth. The material of her dress was a fine silk. She savoured the juice of the fruit. She took her seat.

As soon as the female puppet appeared on stage, her eyes huge and innocent, as if she was just born in that moment, Lucy knew what was going to happen. She pulled her hair over her face. She rummaged urgently in her handbag for her cotton wool but before she got it in her ears, she heard the first line of the puppet's monologue.

It was too late, too early, too late.

She sat in the dark of the theatre, and watched the action like it was a silent movie. The puppet didn't scream but lay there, maggots crawling around her, shadows dancing on the walls baring their teeth and claws. Despite Lucy's distress, she knew her entire life had been leading to this moment, watching it again except this time as a witness. She felt like it had never stopped happening, that somewhere it was always happening and here, finally, was the proof. She couldn't hear the words onstage but she knew they were wrong. That's not how it was, she wanted to say. She gripped the sides of her seat, tore into the armrests as if they were the skin of a fruit.

As the puppet swallowed the abortion pills, fake blood pooling around its body, her face broke apart, the planes separating. The blood was made out of a lumpy, carpet-like substance and appeared when her boyfriend pulled a string. When the puppet was finished, its body slumped on a chair, the lights down, Lucy covered her ears with her hands. She knew people wouldn't clap for that. *Nobody* would clap for that.

Around her, people got to their feet and put their hands together, and she felt a long trail of urine move down her leg. How could you have done it? How could you? It was exactly like the first time, the illusion was gone, she knew again what the world was capable of. She could no longer be the person she had been.

Outside the theatre, a woman asked Lucy if she was alright.

'That was brave, politically,' the woman said, shaking her curls. 'Are you okay?'

'I'm cold,' Lucy said, 'I'm very cold. Was it always this cold?'

'Sweetheart, you're not wearing a coat. It's October.'

Lucy laughed. 'I haven't worn a coat in months.' She paused. 'Can I have yours?'

'My coat?'

'Yes, I need it.'

The woman slowly slipped off her green wool coat.

Lucy took it and started to run.

'Where are you going?' the woman shouted.

When she got to the computer house it was as if she had been running for miles.

She sent an email to the professor.

'Put a large sum of money in my account,' she instructed him, 'and I will make it worth your while when I get back.'

She watched the screen flicker and change in front of her, vaguely registering that it too was a brand. She felt no compulsion to steal it. Outside the computer house she heard a noise, a gentle tap-tap. When she looked around, she saw a girl throwing pebbles at the glass. At first, Lucy thought the girl was trying to get someone's attention inside but then she realised she was directing all her anger at the computer house. The girl stood still, glaring at the computer house for a few more seconds before she disappeared into the night.

'Who was that person?' Lucy asked the boy on the monitor next to her.

'Oh,' he answered, rolling his eyes. 'That's Natasha. I'm not even sure she knows that she comes here. She's a sort of a strange, angry person.'

'So am I.' Lucy stared at the blank screen. 'Well, I'm going now.'

'Where are you going?'

'I'm going on holidays.'

*

She got a taxi to the airport. At the desk she asked for a ticket to any cheap, sunny place.

'Miss, your card has been declined.'

She offered them another card.

'This has also been declined.'

She offered them her final card.

'That worked.'

Her ticket said 'Spain.' In the duty-free she shoplifted a pair of sunglasses. She made a note of the brand in her notebook, and then threw her notebook in the bin. She shoplifted a leopard-print bikini, slipped off her silk dress and piss-soaked knickers and flushed them down the toilet. She climbed into the bikini, closed the respectable wool coat over it and laced up her boots over her bare legs. She reapplied her eye make-up so no one would know that she had been crying. She took a picture, a final picture, in the fluorescent bathroom light. Leaning against the cubicle doors, she rang her boyfriend. He answered after three rings. She could hear his hesitation.

'I'm sorry,' he said, 'I'm so sorry. I wanted to tell your story because I love you.'

'You think that's love? That's not love.'

She hung up and turned her phone off. She took a plastic knife from a coffee shop and jammed it in the back of her phone. She sat in the departure lounge and dismantled her phone piece by piece. She dropped the pieces in the bin. This pleased her greatly. She placed her sunglasses over her eyes and the lounge looked unnatural. Around her everyone sat, waiting for life to begin again. Under her sunglasses, the seats turned orange.

'I'm going on holidays,' she informed the businesslike woman sitting opposite her, engrossed in her screen.

'That's nice,' the woman smiled at her. 'You're free.'

'I'm free.'

On the flight she had a gin and tonic with lime. She squashed the lime up and put it in her pocket as if she might need it for later. As they flew above her country, she watched it become a green dot and imagined squashing it up and putting it in her pocket. On the flight, it felt like the plane might separate – metal springing into the sky – and she would be scooped up into the air. She could take the plane apart with a plastic knife. Her feet landed on tarmac, a flat open plain, a prairie.

She found the worst hotel. She walked right in and asked the man at the reception desk, 'Are there a lot of lost souls in this hotel?' The receptionist said there definitely were. The place was made entirely of concrete, a tower of grey tracing the sky with a half glimpse of the sea available from every room. She threw down her remaining credit card. She was giving herself a week. It was a cement shithole and she felt at home.

In the corridor and in the lift to her room, she saw some of the other lost souls; their faces creased, their lives out of control. They all carried the same look of exhaustion. The women wore bikinis as uniform. She saluted them and their secrets, their hidden illnesses, their scars, the strings that disappeared into their flesh, every decision that led them here, paying for rooms by the hour, by the day, by the week, unable to plan any further. She would keep their secrets. She would shower in the same bathrooms, sleep in the same beds.

The hotel had its own invisible set of rules. No questions. No promises. No bullshit. She lay on her bed and watched the fan, its propellers slicing through the ceiling, cutting the love out of her with every single turn. On her balcony she heard screams of joy. She looked at the sea beyond. She considered the possibility, because of the hotel, that it could be full of sewage. She ran down onto the beach, threw off her coat and jumped in anyway. She took a mouthful of salt water. It was the clearest water she'd ever swam in.

She floated for a long time until the stars appeared, as if being blasted out by a hidden hand. It felt like they should have been accompanied by noise. She wanted noise. She put on her coat and went to a club, a dark purple place where she danced and sweated and spoke to no one. She drank vodka slushies, watermelon, strawberry. She let the ice numb her mouth, dribble onto her body. Hands found her in the dark. She awoke in the morning on her bathroom floor, the green coat stretched over her body like a heavy sheet of seaweed.

Over the next few days, on white deckchairs, sunglasses still fixed to her face, she read books that had been left behind by the other lost souls; books with bad language, with themes of adventure, sticky from the sun. She was sticky from the sun. She rubbed aloe vera into her sunburn. She turned over onto her side. She ate hotdogs, ketchup oozing out, cocktail umbrellas swept up in her wet hair. She threw her body over inflatable animals and let them carry her through the sea. One day she happened upon a funfair – deserted, unsafe. She went on a machine that spun her in convoluted circles on a leather seat. She felt sick with chaos. She thought her head might fall off. When she stepped off, she threw up.

'I would like to go again,' she told the man operating the machine and put down coins.

Every night, she went to a different club, each one a whole new solar system. She did complicated dancing. The music was loud, harsh and she knew it as the music from her past – music of abandoned houses, no parental supervision, reckless parties. She threw back electric colour after electric colour. The stamps of the clubs remained on her wrists all week, unwashed by the seawater. She re-adjusted her bikini in the dark. It was nylon. One night, she met a stag party and, without knowing why, stayed with them for hours. They cut up lines and shared them with her.

'I'm in exile,' she shouted over the music.

They nodded as if this was profound.

She woke up that morning, the Wednesday, in a heap on her balcony. She was really, despite the sun, attached to the green coat, especially now it came with extra layers of dirt.

On her fifth day, she went to the hotel buffet. She had her first taste of a fizzy drink that was close to champagne. 'This,' she announced seriously to an empty room, 'is all I will ever drink now.' That morning she woke up on the cement of her bed beside a man she had no recollection of meeting.

'Are you having a good holiday?' she asked.

'I work here.'

It was the receptionist. He took her out in his beat-up car. She pushed the seat back and stuck her head out the window. She watched the sun set, sitting on a rock.

'It's so beautiful on earth,' she said. 'I haven't seen much of the outside world.'

'Have you been in prison?'

'Sort of.'

She waded out into the water. It was clearer even than the water outside the hotel. 'I'm trying to figure out who I am,' she shouted back at the receptionist.

The receptionist thought for a while. Lucy could see him thinking on the rock. 'I have to get back to the desk now,' he said.

That night, her second last, she walked home from the club through the crowds and rubbish-filled streets. All the apartments looked broken down; the town was angry and tense. It looked like a mouth with teeth removed. She went for a burger. She chose an option from the menu above her head, laid out in flat illustration. She spent a long time at the till. When she sat down an older man caught her eye. His face said, 'I just want to talk to you. What's wrong with that?'

'What are you doing here?' he asked.

'I'm on holidays.'

'What are you really doing here?'

Lucy put down her food. 'I'm letting my life fall apart.'

There was something demonic about him. He had shimmied out of a dark corner somewhere. His reflection seemed to move around the restaurant.

'That's more like it,' he said.

Outside on the street, amid the giggles and the shrieks and the dull noise, she bent over with stomach cramps. She bought a bottle of vodka, opened all the doors and windows in her hotel room and listened to the other lost souls, pounding away above and below her. The lift moved up and down, letting people in and out. She thought about waking up beside her ex. Even when she wasn't thinking about him, she was thinking about him. She thought about waking up alone. She thought about not waking up at all. She passed out as the voices continued to float up to her room.

Her last night she went to the hotel buffet. She spread a napkin across her lap. She asked the receptionist for paper and a pen. She stayed in and sat on the wire chair on her balcony. The heat was immovable; it was a wall. There was a storm starting. She could feel it in the heat. Reality was thinner in heat like this. The light reflected different shapes on the concrete. On every floor people moved around, fleeing or preparing to return to their mangled lives. On the top of the first sheet of hotel paper she wrote, 'My life is my own.' She remembered the model-box, the world pulled from her boyfriend's imagination. She knew she could keep doing this, or some version of this for the rest of her life, but it wouldn't be freedom and she wanted freedom. If you wanted a place that was lawless, you had to invent it yourself.

She was making her mind up in a way she had never done before. She was leaving a part of herself behind. She knew if she was going to do it, she would have to do it all. That night, on the hotel stationery, she started her first play. It would be about suffering; it would be about survival. It would be proof that she was alive. It would star two girls. It would be called: *Abortion, A Love Story*.

PUTTING ON A SHOW

'Can I start over?'

Lucy was auditioning for a play and Natasha sat three rows from the back, watching her. Her chest was tight. Onstage Lucy was doing some approximation of walking, but the floor wasn't responding to her touch. The floor was against her. Natasha wondered how all Lucy's gifts had vanished. She looked like she was contemplating a problem up there and that problem was herself. She was the worst actress Natasha had ever seen. It was distressing to witness this performance.

A member of the acting troupe coughed. The acting troupe were infamous in the college: two boys and a singular girl, each of them dark-haired and intense, they stalked around as if they were in possession of a secret, unbearable knowledge of the outside world. Natasha thought they were pretentious assholes. They owned three sets of high cheekbones and came from acting dynasties. Their Shakespearean deconstructions were set in asylums and all they did, from what Natasha could tell, was grind their teeth. As if that's all madness was: grinding your teeth. In these productions, the girl was always tied extravagantly with ropes. The ropes symbolised her lack of sexual freedom. The few minutes of these performances that Natasha had caught had depressed her beyond all reason.

Offstage, the girl slithered around the college, her eyes narrowed into slits, her mouth furious, as if expecting a sea to part for her, a seismic shift in the universe that would restore her to her rightful place. All three were rumoured to be in a tempestuous relationship, arguing loudly in the college coffee shop over what sounded like grim, selfish sex. Natasha's gaze flitted from Lucy to check from their body language who was sleeping with who today. They were auditioning actresses for their latest project and Natasha had persuaded them to try Lucy. Natasha could tell, from their backs, that they were unimpressed. They wanted Lucy to be grateful for this opportunity. Lucy wasn't grateful. Natasha suspected she had never been grateful in her life. She didn't know how.

'Can I start over?' Lucy asked again.

'Fine,' the lead actor intoned, bored. He was a legendary piece of work

Lucy disappeared behind the curtain and re-emerged in a pure white nightdress.

'Why are you wearing that?' the girl-actor asked.

'It signifies the mental state of my character,' Lucy explained, 'which is destructive.'

'Just say your name and where you're from.'

'I'm Lucy.'

'And where are you from?'

'I don't know where I'm from.'

Natasha laughed. The troupe turned to look at her, three serious faces. 'She really doesn't know where she's from,' Natasha said, 'just let her start.'

Lucy moved behind the table as if to begin her monologue. She looked at the table for a few minutes. She started making choo-choo noises, performing the motion of a train with her arms.

'What's that?' the piece of work asked.

'That's the start.'

'No, it's not.'

'That's how I've interpreted the start of this woman's sad journey,' Lucy explained.

'Just say the monologue,' the girl interrupted. 'Say the lines as you've learnt them.'

'Okay,' Lucy agreed, but didn't supply anything further. There was a short silence. 'Can I start again?' she asked.

'Jesus Christ,' the shortest, most aggressive actor shouted.

'Just let her try again,' Natasha pleaded from the back.

'What is wrong with you?' the girl-actor asked Lucy, genuinely interested.

'I'm here to audition,' Lucy replied haughtily, 'not for a character assessment.'

'Okay, go then.'

Lucy hid behind the curtain. Natasha could see her fluttery, desperate movements.

She walked out unsteadily wearing a stained dressing-gown and carrying a whiskey glass.

'What's that?' The short actor rubbed his hand across his face in weariness.

'It's a drink. If I know this particular character she would need a drink at a time like this. To assist with her illusions and keep reality at bay.'

'What's a time like this?'

'A time of despair and pitiful loneliness.'

'Has she put her dressing-gown on because of despair?' Natasha could hear the sneer in the girl-actor's voice. It came naturally to her, like birdsong.

'No,' Lucy said, 'she's put her dressing-gown on because she's cold.'

'Just begin. Please begin.'

'Okay,' Lucy agreed.

'Is that actual whiskey in that glass?'

Lucy nodded.

'Put it down.'

Lucy put down the glass. 'Do you want me to pick up anything else in its place?'

'No. Just begin.'

'Fine.'

Lucy paused.

'I've forgotten, do you want me to pick up the glass or put it down?'

'Put it down.' The piece of work said each word slowly, as if communicating with a child.

Lucy perched herself at the edge of the table and rested her chin on her knuckles.

'Thank you for the flowers,' Lucy said.

'There are no flowers in this play,' the short actor said.

'I love the flowers you've brought me, but I must comport myself like a woman and say no.'

'There are no flowers!'

Lucy was holding an imaginary bunch of flowers in her right hand. 'Are these lilies?'

Natasha watched the girl-actor, waiting for her to say something. Instead, she was leaning forward, her body bobbing back and forth. She was laughing. Lucy had made this professional mourner laugh.

'It's just I read the whole play,' Lucy said, 'and I thought this woman has been through a lot. Why not give her a bunch of flowers?'

'Right,' the short actor said.

'You don't like it,' Lucy said. 'You don't like it. Let me go again.'

The two male actors looked traumatised.

Lucy grabbed the flesh of her face. 'Soon I will grow old and die,' she announced.

'Are you saying that or is the character saying that?' the short actor asked, as if at least trying to understand.

'Oh both,' Lucy said. 'Both. I can declare it's true. It's something I learned on my recent exploration and discovery of myself, far away from here, far away from this college.'

'Where did you go?'

'Spain.'

The girl-actor wiped away tears of mirth as Lucy, once more, stumbled behind the curtain. In that moment Natasha realised something, something so obvious she couldn't believe it had taken her this long. She gathered up her bag and the papers on her lap. She stood up.

'Thank you,' she said to the troupe, as she exited. 'I used to think you were all incredible assholes, but you're not so bad. Please tell Lucy when she's finished to meet me in the coffee shop.'

When she left the theatre she heard a glass smash. 'It's so hard to behave like a lady,' Lucy screamed in a southern accent.

*

That night they met in the restaurant, after they had said goodbye to Professor Carr, kissing him on each cheek, making vague promises, Lucy and Natasha ran together through the city streets. What was happening to the city? Glass covered every millimetre. There were no faces, only glass. Natasha could hardly believe, in only two months, she would be expected to live in it forever.

Lucy's apartment was full to the brim with colourful stuff, tiny handbags, bottles with labels identifying the style of scent, exercise equipment, beautification tools Natasha had never seen before. Nothing looked touched. It was as if there had been a reverse burglary. Lucy lay on her bed and seated Natasha beside her.

'You know what I thought when I first saw you with the professor?'

'What?'

'I thought: there goes a real idiot.'

'I see.'

'And I had a crisis of conscience. Should I tell her she's an idiot? Maybe she doesn't know?'

'That was thoughtful of you.'

'I got hopelessly sucked into your emails.'

'It was rude of you to read my emails.'

'They were very compelling.'

'Good, I suppose.'

'And I figured I got you wrong. I like the clips your dad sends you. Did you write them?'

'They are from television.'

'I like books,' Lucy said, airily. 'Quotes.'

'Oh.'

'You don't sound excited by books.'

Natasha was quiet.

Lucy flipped onto her stomach and held up an imaginary clipboard.

'When I saw you outside the computer house,' Lucy said, 'your hair everywhere, spitting, throwing stones at the building, I couldn't describe the feelings I had.'

'No?'

'I felt like I had finally found my artistic equal.'

'I don't really like art.'

'That doesn't make any difference.'

'Okay.'

'What was dating the professor like?'

Natasha eyed a pile of perfumes that looked like it might topple over. Glasses of different sizes and shapes, an unwieldy pyramid, with notes in similar handwriting attached to each lid. 'Brutal, unforgiving,' Natasha replied. 'He kept making me watch films of a high cultural standard.'

'Why did you do it?' Lucy made a note on her imaginary chart.

'I do things and I don't know why I do them.'

'Were you in love with him?'

'No.'

'I was in love before,' Lucy said sadly. 'But it was over like that.' She clicked her fingers.

'I'm sorry.'

'I called him once when I was drunk from a payphone near my hotel.'

'Oh no.'

'And he answered and I said: "Relax, stay on the line. Stay on the line. I'm not going to say anything mean."'

'And?'

'I said something mean.'

'What did you say?'

'I couldn't repeat it.' Lucy looked away. 'It's that shocking. It wouldn't be right if I told you. No one will ever know what was said on that payphone.'

'Obscenities?'

'Things are said when you drink.' Lucy cleared her throat. 'Would you admit to having self-destructive impulses?'

Natasha nodded. 'I would admit that.'

'Would you say that you're a typical Irish girl?'

'I would say I'm not a typical anything.'

'Where is your home?

'I could point it out on a map but I don't know really.'

'How do you feel about this college?'

'I feel every day,' Natasha said, 'that I'm in the process of losing a long and complicated bet, one that will carry on for several years, where I will end up down a huge amount of money.'

'Is that a secret you've never told anybody before?'

'Yes.'

Lucy swung her legs over the side of her bed. She had tiny, well-manicured feet. The room seemed to reverberate, the walls shaking, the perfumes emitting all their scents at once. 'Would you say that you're a complete liability in almost every respect?'

'I have a lot of self-control,' Natasha said, as if it were her final prayer.

'Would you say that you're a complete liability in almost every respect?' Lucy repeated.

Natasha looked at Lucy's tiny feet. How had she walked across the world on those? She cast her memory over her life. She saw certain scenes. 'It's possible I have no self-control. None at all,' she said, finally.

'Hold on.' Lucy jumped off her bed. 'I will be back.'

When Lucy was gone, Natasha examined the inscriptions on the perfume bottles. It was Professor Carr's handwriting on every single one. The emotion she felt most overwhelmingly was pity.

Lucy walked back in carrying a thick, brown envelope. 'This is my life's work,' she said. 'I wrote it in a hot foreign country when I was having a life-changing experience. I believe it's the result of visions. I want you to read it and then we will perform it together in the college theatre. It is important to me.' She closed her eyes. 'I can't imagine we will be the same after it's finished.' She drew the envelope close to her chest, as if saying goodbye to it, and then thrust it at Natasha.

'Do you want me to read it now?'

'I must warn you,' Lucy said, 'it's not a healthy work. I was heartbroken when I wrote it. It might unnerve you.'

Natasha shook the envelope.

'It might make you question everything you know.'

Natasha sat down.

'You can't read it here,' Lucy said. 'I don't want to hear the conversation you have with it.'

Natasha left and walked back through the city in the early morning sunshine. She bought a small cup of coffee and strolled in the direction of the library. Natasha had avoided the library since the early days of first year when she had interrupted the tour guide to ask if the building was an 'antique' and the group had laughed at her. She tried to relax now, going back in, but her mouth felt dry and thirsty. When she thought of all the knowledge that had been gathered there, all the expensive jackets that had been carelessly draped on the backs of chairs, all the minds seeking Truth, she felt sick. She hurried to the first floor before she could back out.

The place was empty except for one boy, his head buried in a heavy book. He was sniffling and wiping his nose on the back of his hand. Natasha stared at him. 'College,' she said, as if it had just been invented, as if she had invented it. She rolled her eyes to indicate her workload. The boy only buried his head further in his book, his loud snuffles cracking the silence.

Natasha took a seat near the studious boy and began examining Lucy's play. She slid it out from its envelope. It was written on hotel stationery and long sections were illegible. On every page Lucy had crossed out the name of the hotel and written 'Hotel of Lost Souls' instead. On some pages the play veered into room service orders. It appeared to have been written in great haste. Several of the pages were damp from the sea or had gin spilled on them. In the margins Lucy had left little notes for herself like 'I don't know what I'm doing here!'

The play itself was a chore – no spirit, no excitement, no life. The exact opposite of Lucy. It was an extensive history of Irish women played by two female characters. Every time you thought you got rid of them, they pulled themselves up and gasped another agonising breath. Several sections were written in verse for a Greek chorus. There were scenes where women rose out of the soil; a scene where the two girls lay face down on carpets. The play couldn't accommodate all the misery that was in it. Natasha felt greyer after finishing it. She took out a red pen and begin drawing lines through sentences, rearranging words. An hour passed before she realised what she was doing.

'I know how to do this,' she said, in shock. 'How do I know how to do this?'

The boy looked up and gave his most elaborate sniff yet.

'I'm trying to study,' he said.

'That won't help you in life,' Natasha said, with weary finality. 'You should stand up, put your pricey jacket on and walk the streets.'

'I will call the library police.'

Natasha left the library with *Abortion, A Love Story* tucked under her arm, the sheets ruffling in the wind. She knew she couldn't perform the play with Lucy. They would be laughing stocks. She thought about the most sensitive way to tell her. She rang the doorbell to Lucy's student house but there was no answer. She knelt down and called into the letterbox.

'Lucy.'

She knew Lucy was leaning on the other side of the door.

'Lucy,' she said, 'I've just been to the library.'

'That place is an antique,' Lucy said, softly.

'I want to praise your play. I liked its anger. I liked in the second act when the women call the college a prison. I think you've done a tremendous job. You said everything you need to say, in language that sometimes makes sense. And the completion of great work is its own reward. You don't need to take it any further. You came close. It's enough to know you nearly got there. '

Lucy opened the door. Her hair was wild and her face was tear-stained. 'No,' she said. 'It's not enough. Why isn't it enough?'

Natasha knew just from looking at her, that this was a woman in the grip of a great dependency. 'Let's see what we can do,' she said.

*

Natasha thought Lucy's particular urge might be satisfied by acting in a play instead. She went to the computer house and emailed the acting troupe to tell them about Lucy's tiny feet, shoplifting addiction and periods of mania. They said they were very interested in her coming on board. For two weeks, the girls immersed themselves in plays to find a monologue that Lucy could audition with. It was March and there were no seats in the library. Just looking around gave Natasha palpitations. They took off their jackets and lay on the floor.

In the plays, there were women walking in and out of doors, women calling their husbands for dinner, women staying faithful to their husbands, or being unfaithful and getting severely punished for it; women who lived on islands, lonely women or women who wanted to be left alone, plain women, watchful women and, frequently, dead women. Throughout, Natasha kept *Abortion, A Love Story* in an envelope beside her. She couldn't leave it. She thought it might reveal something to her.

'Here,' Natasha said, one Wednesday afternoon, sliding a script over to Lucy. 'I think you should audition with this.'

Lucy read through it. 'This woman seems delusional and unstable.'

'She is delusional and unstable,' Natasha said. 'It's perfect.'

Now, Natasha waited in the college coffee shop for Lucy to return from her ill-fated audition. She had the pages of *Abortion, A Love Story* spread out in front of her. She watched Lucy enter the coffee shop in a huff. She took a fizzy drink from the fridge and slammed the door shut. She pulled out the seat opposite Natasha.

'I don't like that acting troupe at all,' she said. 'They pretend to be the gatekeepers of something. What the hell are they the gatekeepers of?' She stabbed her drink with her straw. 'Tell me. Be honest. Was I bad up there?'

'Lucy,' Natasha said, holding up a page covered in red marks, 'let's make this a comedy.'

'*Abortion, A Love Story*?'

Natasha nodded.

'But it's about these two girls, sisters in misery.'

'I know.'

'They don't have anything.'

'Of course.'

'It's a bad time.

'It's a woeful time.'

'And it gets worse.'

'How?'

'It's always raining.'

'True.'

Lucy took a sip of her drink. 'Who could find all that funny?'

'Not me.'

'And the pain and the suffering of the women,' Lucy said, shaking her head. 'The violence of what they have endured. That's what the audience will want.'

'Yeah,' Natasha said, 'and let's not give it to them.'

Lucy was silent.

'Comedy is tragedy sped up.'

Lucy tapped two fingers on her can. 'That's Ionesco.'

'I thought it was my dad,' Natasha said.

'You know we're risking our reputations.'

'We don't have reputations to risk.' Natasha leaned forward. 'Do you trust me, Lucy?'

Lucy took a long, thoughtful gulp. She nodded.

*

The room where they worked was an abandoned class-room at the back of the college, and they spent every available minute in there. The first day Lucy arrived dressed up, wearing a pretty cardigan and shirt. She looked like someone who believed in order.

'Take that off,' Natasha instructed. 'There's no room for order here.'

They spent all that first day in the room working out the shape and texture of the play. They stretched. They meditated. They rubbed crystals that Lucy had stolen. They played inspiring music. Should they start, elementally, as trees swaying in the breeze? Should they crawl from the dirt? Should they monologue their feelings? Should their characters have good intentions?

'Let's not do the obvious thing,' Natasha said.

After that, they didn't say anything for a long time. In the evening, they sat together in the computer house and watched the old comedy clips that Natasha's father had collected – men flying off ladders, through hatch doors, men whose cars wouldn't start, men whose businesses were failing, men being thwarted at every turn – a black and white stream of men getting energetically angry. The clips, all strung together manically, were the opposite of culture, the opposite of civilised behaviour and reason. These clowns with their bright red faces were the radical opposite of beauty. There was nothing discreet in these clips, everything was loud and frantic. They were somehow good and bad at the same time.

'Can we get gin and tonics?' Lucy whispered.

It took Lucy several days to turn the full focus of her attention to the clips but when she did, Natasha couldn't believe what she could retain. Specific gestures, movements, costumes – there was nothing that escaped her attention. She recited punchlines word for word. Her mind, which couldn't handle one bit of reality, could hold the imaginative world. To rouse themselves out of their creative stupor, they talked about what they were fighting against – earnestness of any kind, the dry, the humourless. Boredom, Lucy added. Logic. Moral dictation.

'Why did you write this play in the first place?'

'I wanted a place that was lawless,' Lucy said.

'No laws.' Natasha made a little note of it in her notebook. Her notebook now had two notes in it and a convoluted sketch of a man falling off a ladder.

Outside the window was a large oak tree and Lucy often looked at its gently moving branches as Natasha had a nervous breakdown. On dry days, as it came into April, and fourth year students planned their graduation into the outside world, where buildings were razed and felled and businessmen were routinely accused of improper dealings, Lucy and Natasha stuck cotton wool in their ears and lay under the tree. Occasionally Professor Carr appeared and looked at them baldly across the green, sickened by their new, unholy alliance.

'Shoo,' Lucy shouted and they watched him scamper away.

The pages somehow built up. They stayed late. They worked Sundays. Their giggles could be heard in other rooms in the building. The play slowly jerked to life. Lines were written. Ideas were formed. In the beginning their ambition was huge and they talked about setting it in a house with a chandelier, bringing it down in a massive crash at the end of the first act. The chandelier would represent the college. It would symbolise the end of a regime. But they had no money and they had no chandelier. They had no money at all. They had to be economical. They were using the last few cents in Lucy's account.

'The chandelier would have been excessive anyway,' Lucy said. 'Ostentatious.'

'We don't need a chandelier,' Natasha said, 'we're making a new reality.'

'It would have been nice though.'

'Satisfying, for sure.'

'That smash,' Lucy smacked her hand on the table. 'Glass everywhere.'

'Beautiful.'

Neither of them knew how to sew. Lucy learned by watching videos in the computer house, her fingers moving in and out of the material nimbly. All the clothes came out at strange angles. They were immensely weird in a way neither Lucy or Natasha could explain, all oddly improvised: staples where trouser tucks should be, sellotape everywhere.

'This works better,' Natasha decided.

On an evening in their third week, the tree stretching out ominously in the dark, Natasha looked up from the delicate arrangement of safety pins she was working on. She hadn't seen the inside of a lecture theatre in several months. She no longer knew how the chairs were arranged; she was even losing the slight amount of knowledge she had gained in Professor Carr's office.

'I am going to the unemployment building,' she said.

Lucy looked at her intently. 'You are,' she said. 'You're going to the unemployment building, you will see the rotting walls, you will count the cracks in the ceiling, you will join the long lines, you will sit in a plastic seat with your number to receive a nonexistent amount of income.'

'Will it be as bad as we've all imagined it to be?'

'You will cry but, for the sake of appearances, you will hide it in your sleeve. You will close your eyes and pretend to be elsewhere.'

'But I won't be elsewhere.'

'No.'

'Where will I be?'

'You will be in the unemployment building.'

'So be it,' Natasha said, with great strength, as if facing up to a prophecy.

'I will be alone here without you.'

Lucy and Natasha had grown so close over the last few weeks, it felt like they had become one fast and vicious animal. Natasha learned all of Lucy's lines; Lucy learned all of Natasha's lines. They knew when the other was going to move; they could predict it and they moved together. There was no impulse that was wrong. When it became dark, when the oak tree became slick and shiny with rain, they stayed inside and talked about growing up as unenlightened children; life on country roads, holidays on stony beaches under grey skies, their homes, the prison of their homes. They talked about everything, everything distasteful and rotten and shameful about their lives. They tore the skin off it. They found beauty in it; they put it all in the play. And they would laugh at it. They would reveal it and they would laugh at it.

'I will come back and see you,' Natasha said.

'After this, Natasha, they're not going to let you in the front gate.'

*

It was their last week and they were outside painting scenery when a boy pulled up beside them on a bicycle. He had sandy hair and a look of supreme disinterest. Natasha could see a single, waxy puppet hand poking out of his schoolbag.

'Take it back,' he said to Lucy.

'No,' Lucy said, without looking at him, 'I will never take it back.'

'Take it back,' he screamed.

'No,' Lucy roared.

'You cunt.' He jumped up on his bicycle and they watched him wobble away. They watched him for a few minutes as he bumped over the cobblestones. There were several severe bumps.

'That's him anyway,' Natasha said.

'That's him.'

'What did you say to him?'

'I told him he was never good enough for me.'

Natasha watched as he struggled to straighten himself on his bicycle. 'That's objectively true,' she said, 'you can't argue with that.'

'And I said something awful.'

'What?'

'Imagine the worst thing you can say to a man like that.'

'You called him a mediocrity.'

'Worse.' Lucy whispered into Natasha's ear. She spoke for a short time.

Natasha's face broke out into a huge smile. 'Let's put that in the play.'

*

The night before Lucy and Natasha submitted the play to the student theatre, Natasha had a dream that her mother rang her up out of the blue. The phone she answered was not her own. She was in a long hallway with a lot of different rooms. She had no idea which room the call was coming from. When she told her mother she hadn't had an absolutely brilliant childhood, her mother laughed and said, 'Your father could have been better, yes.' When she awoke, she felt sure it was a sign that the play was going to be a tremendous success. That morning, she and Lucy walked to the college together. Lucy wore a pair of huge sunglasses and kept bumping into things and apologising. They had to cross the campus to the theatre. It was the longest walk ever.

'Let me go up,' Lucy said, as they stood at the bottom of the stairs. 'I'm charming.'

'I can be charming.'

Lucy stood on the bottom step. 'But I'm more so. Today, I'm more so.' She walked up.

She re-appeared five minutes later. 'He said no. It's over.'

'How much did he read?'

'The first page.'

Lucy sighed. She kicked a small pot containing a dying shrub. 'Maybe it's enough.'

Natasha took the pages out of her hand. 'It's not enough.'

Upstairs, in the low-ceilinged room, sat a boy, thumbing through a novel.

'You're right,' Natasha said. 'It's bad.'

He didn't look up.

'But I don't care,' Natasha continued. 'Give us one night.'

'The acting troupe are in there for the next two weeks,' he said, and continued lazily turning the pages, 'and then college is over.'

Natasha thought of the starchy graduation robes. The rushed and formal ceremony that she would not be welcome at anyway. Only the boy's presence kept her from vomiting.

'One night,' she said.

'The acting troupe are in there for the next two weeks. You will have to fight them for it.' He looked her up and down. 'Are you willing to do that?'

Natasha took the book out of his hand and cleared herself a space at the edge of his desk. She knocked over several papers and pens. 'I know you want me to go away,' she said.

The boy looked scared.

'But let me tell you about where I grew up.'

A week later the chalkboard at the front of the theatre read:

Abortion, A Love Story: One Night Only.

*

In the hour before the show, Natasha and Lucy sat in the changing room, sharing a cake. They divided the cake into thin slices, which Natasha didn't touch. A bottle of Lucy's beloved fizzy drink also remained sweating on the table.

'I feel like I'm being smothered,' Natasha said.

'It's just nerves,' Lucy replied.

'I think somebody has cut off my oxygen supply.'

'Nerves. You're nervous.'

'I'm not.'

'Don't let them see it,' Lucy said, popping a slice of cake into her mouth. Natasha could see the pink icing beneath her tongue. 'That's important. Don't let them see it.'

An hour earlier before they'd unpacked their props and organised themselves, they had exchanged flowers, cards and well wishes. On Natasha's card, Lucy had written:

'If we were in a long banquet hall filled with the world's best and most interesting people, I would only want to sit beside you. Lucy x.' On Lucy's card Natasha had written, 'Best of luck with the play!' which was the level of emotion she was capable of expressing at the time.

The boy from the theatre walked into the dressing room. He avoided Natasha and directed his gaze towards the palm tree in the corner. 'This is your five-minute call.'

'How many people are out there?' Lucy asked.

'Ten.' The boy looked at his clipboard. 'At last count.'

'That's too many,' Natasha said, 'we should ask some of them to leave.'

'She's nervous,' Lucy explained.

The boy nodded and indicated for them to follow him. As they walked down the hall, Lucy said, 'If you mess up out there, just blame it on me. Give me a dirty look or whatever.'

'I don't think I'm going to go on,' Natasha said abruptly as they reached the curtain.

Natasha could see the acting troupe in the first row, their gazes critical, their posture somehow both angry and indifferent. The sight of them disturbed her. The rest of the audience was dark.

'You have to go on.'

'I don't think there's any need to. I really don't think there's any need to.'

'I'm counting you in. Five, four … '

Lucy looked at Natasha. She thought of her sitting alone in a cafe in the city. She thought of her in the unemployment building, her legs swinging on a metal seat. She knew she didn't want to go out there. Just her taking one step onto that stage was a declaration of love.

'Natasha.'

Natasha's eyes didn't move off the stage.

'I love you,' Lucy said. The lights hit Natasha's face. 'You're on.'

SHOWTIME

Natasha walks onstage wearing her own clothes. She stands in the middle of the stage. From a megaphone offstage, Lucy calls out, 'Natasha, welcome to the unemployment building.'

'Thank you for having me,' Natasha says.

'Your number is 32. There is nothing to do except cooperate, do you understand?'

'I understand.'

'Under disabilities, you've listed a non-specific disorder.'

'Yes,' Natasha says.

'Under employment history, you've listed none.'

'That's correct.'

'Under reason you can't work you've written: "I'm tired of acting normal."'

'That came to me after a considered assessment.'

'Natasha, you have to do things our way.'

'No,' Natasha says.

'No?' Lucy bellows.

'No.'

'You won't do things our way?'

Out of the corner of her eye, Natasha can see Lucy pulling on her costume, the megaphone in her right hand.

'Not tonight,' Natasha says. 'Tonight you're doing things our way.'

The lights go down.

'Ladies and gentlemen, it's my great pleasure to introduce Lucy.'

Natasha disappears behind the curtain and pulls Lucy out on a chaise longue on wheels. Lucy is wearing a fluffy, see-through robe over a pink negligee. She is sprawled across the couch and is holding an old-style telephone in her hand. She rests on her left elbow, facing the audience.

'Oh baby, I know, I know,' Lucy says into the telephone. 'Oh I know, it's awful to be so in love. I will see what I'm doing on Saturday.'

She puts down the phone. It starts ringing again, urgently, a high, shrill sound. Lucy slips on a pair of pom-pom slippers and answers. 'I will see what I'm doing Saturday,' she says. 'It's hard to be so in love, but you will relax into it, you will get used to it. That's my advice.'

She puts down the phone and pushes a lock of hair out of her face. 'My phone never stops ringing,' she says to the audience. 'That's just the way it is.'

The phone rings again. 'I will see what I'm doing Saturday,' she says, more briskly this time. She puts the phone down and stares into space. 'My phone never stops ringing,' she says, almost despairing.

The phone rings again. 'I will see what I'm doing Saturday,' she says, robotically. She places down the receiver. 'I like the cocktails and the compliments.'

The phone rings again. Each ring is louder, angrier. 'I will see what I'm doing Saturday,' she screams and puts down the receiver. 'I like the cocktails and the compliments, but after a while it all starts to turn my stomach.' She twirls a piece of her hair in her finger. There is complete silence.

The phone rings again. 'I will see what I'm doing Saturday,' Lucy says. She re-adjusts her negligee, squeezes her breasts. She listens more carefully. She switches the phone to her other ear. She nods. She stands up and walks around with the phone in her hand. She giggles.

'You earn how much a week? Without tax? So what's your take-home pay? I don't mean to be brash but a woman has to think about these things,' Lucy says. 'I have a right to ask. It's an issue I get pretty heated about. A woman has to think about her place in society. She has to rise. You sound like an upstanding citizen with prospects.' Lucy winks at the audience, a big, exaggerated batting of her right eye. 'So I guess I will come right over.'

Lucy exits with the telephone in her hand, as Natasha drags a carpet onstage. She unrolls it. It is a white woolly material. Natasha wears a dress, a long silver sheath. Before she lies down, she pulls a string and a large screen fills the space behind her.

'I carry this everywhere with me,' Natasha explains to the audience, 'because carpet is still new to me. I grew up in a house that was all hardwood, low-ceilinged, a bungalow on a country road.' Natasha starts laughing. 'I was what you call dirt poor.' She bends over as if this is the funniest thing she has ever heard. 'I won't put you through it; just picture death and you're nearly there. We didn't even have a VCR so I hadn't seen many films before I became an actress. Anyway, enough about me.' She turns her back to the audience and faces the screen. 'Let's watch a film.'

Onscreen, hundreds of clips ran together, moving from black and white to colour. In the clips, women walk in and out of rooms; they are grabbed at by faceless figures. They sprawl on furniture and are photographed: tied to train tracks, being slapped hard across their faces. Hundreds of close-ups of women with tears in their eyes, their features unmoving, their faces all strikingly similar. At the end, a single scene plays again and again: a woman is punched in the face. Blood spurts from her nose as she smiles. 'You love me,' the woman says, as she lies on the floor. 'This means you really love me.' As this scene plays, Natasha pours red liquid all over the carpet until it becomes fully red and filthy, her feet soaked with the liquid.

'What was I saying?' Natasha turns back to face the audience. She is laughing. Some of the liquid gets caught in her hair and runs down her face. She is holding an award. 'I guess I'm just happy to be here,' she says, 'because, despite everything, you guys love me. I mean you really, really love me, don't you?'

She rolls up the carpet and pushes it offstage. She pulls the string and the screen disappears. She picks a sign up from the floor and shows it to the audience. The sign reads: 'The Big Comeback Special.' Natasha exits.

Lucy walks onstage holding a cigarette and a glass of wine. She looks relaxed in jeans and a black T-shirt. She carries a microphone stand under her left arm. She places the stand down and adjusts its height. She taps the microphone. She takes a drag of her cigarette.

'Did you miss me?' she asks into the microphone.

The audience claps.

'You wrote me off, didn't you? That was stupid. You shouldn't have done that.' She takes another drag. 'I'm here to be humorous. It's my "comeback special." They made me call it that. Have you ever heard of anything so dumb?' She rolls her eyes. She exhales and bats the smoke out of her face. She takes a sip of her wine. 'Okay, so a girl walks into a bar,' she says, smiling. 'Wait, that's not right, let me start again.'

Lucy exits. She does a silly little dance as she struts back in. 'Okay, so a girl walks into a bar.' She points her cigarette at the audience. She keeps a smile on her face throughout. 'I know what you're up to. I mean you guys act all innocent, like you just came here to see a girl tell a few jokes, but I'm not so sure about you sick fucks.' The audience laughs, appreciating being called sick fucks. Lucy takes another sip of her wine. She claps her hands.

'So a girl walks into a bar.' She thinks for a few seconds. 'Wait, let me start again.'

Lucy exits and dances back in with a newly lit ciga-rette. 'Okay,' she says, 'I'm ready to go now.' She hits the side of her wine glass. 'It's hot up here, isn't it?' she says, as if it has just occurred to her. 'So what have you guys been up to?' She gestures at the audience. 'Just taking it easy? Relaxing?' She nods. 'Cool. See my problem with all of you, and this has always been my problem, is that I just don't like any of you very much and I never have, you bunch of pricks.' The audience laughs again at the insult. 'I don't think you came out here to hear me be funny at all. I think you came out to hear some pain. You don't care what it is exactly, but you want it. You're so *competitive* about it. And I just think—fuck you, you know.' She takes a long drink. 'You never, ever get tired, do you? You take one look at me and you need to know I've been punished.'

Natasha enters, dressed as a stagehand, and takes the cigarette and drink off Lucy. She puts her hand on Lucy's shoulder before she walks off.

'Well, you asked,' Lucy says. 'You want to know. So here it is.'

She moves to put her hand on the microphone stand, but Natasha swoops in and takes the microphone stand away. Lucy grabs at the microphone before she can take it.

'A girl walks into a house. She's sixteen,' she starts. Natasha returns and takes the microphone out of Lucy's hand. Lucy can't be heard. She starts crying, tears moving down her face. After ten minutes, when Lucy is finished, when her mouth has stopped moving, Natasha walks back onstage with Lucy's cigarette and glass of wine. She readjusts the microphone stand for Lucy's exact height. She puts her arm around Lucy's shoulder before she exits.

Lucy steps up to the microphone.

'For several months, when I was sixteen, I thought I was going to die.' Lucy takes a slow drag. The smoke rises upwards. 'But when I was twenty I sat on a balcony in Spain. A storm was starting, but I didn't move. I could hear the thunder. The rain came down and soaked the paper I was working on. Some of the words ran. And I was so happy.' Lucy pauses. 'For several months when I was sixteen I thought I was going to die.' She smiles, a huge, broad smile. 'But I didn't die.' She stubs out her cigarette. 'And that's it from me tonight, ladies and gentlemen.' She bows. 'That's it from me. It feels so good to be back. Honestly, you have no idea.'

As Lucy exits, Natasha walks onstage holding a wooden desk. She is wearing a school uniform, a blue jumper and tiny, tight blue skirt. She sets the desk down. She puts her feet up. She fixes her hair. She writes something on a sheet of paper.

Lucy glides onstage in a nun's costume. She is wearing a pair of tiny spectacles. She holds a bucket in each hand. She stands still like a statue behind Natasha. She wears an expression of absolute beatification.

'Don't let me stir you from your slumber, my child,' she says, quietly.

Natasha jumps.

'Take your feet down off that desk.'

Natasha puts her feet on the floor.

'Now, my sweet child, you know why I've brought you here today.'

'I think so.'

'You've been accepted into the most elite college. A place apart.'

'I have.'

'Have a sweet in celebration.' Lucy takes a sweet out of her pocket and offers it to Natasha.

Natasha eats the sweet.

'It's an achievement. That's why I gave you a sweet,' Lucy-as-nun explains.

'It is delicious.'

'You're the only girl in your year to go to this elite college. Do you feel any pressure?'

'Not really,' Natasha says.

'Don't tell lies.'

'I'm not lying.'

'Maybe you should,' Lucy-as-nun says, thoughtfully. 'Maybe you should feel some pressure. Hold up the paper. Show everyone your results in the examinations.'

Natasha holds up the paper to the audience.

'Now, my dearest child, those are great marks but don't get ahead of yourself.'

'No,' Natasha says, seriously.

'Don't lose the run of yourself.'

'I won't.'

Lucy-as-nun rests her tiny hands on the side of the desk as if she is interrogating Natasha. She lowers her spectacles. 'Do you promise to leave this place and never look back.'

'I promise, Sister.'

'So you swear to leave this slum, the giant quarry in which you were born, and never to gaze upon it again?'

'I swear, Sister.' Natasha smooths down her skirt as if in preparation.

'Do you promise to rise to moderate heights with a quiet and civilised personality?'

'I do, Sister.'

'Do you swear to find a good man and accompany him to all social occasions where you will have only one single brandy over the course of the evening?'

'I will do that to the best of my abilities, Sister.'

'Now, if you find out your husband has been living a sort of double life and he buys you a car as compensation, what do you say to that?'

'I say: "Is that Unleaded or Diesel?"'

'Very good, my child.' Lucy adjusts her habit and gazes out proudly. 'Now, before you leave this school forever, I'm going to impart some information about college.'

'I would appreciate that, Sister.'

'There is no bell in college. No bell like this.' A school bell screeches out. 'But that doesn't mean you can just stand up and leave whenever you want.'

'No, I agree, Sister.'

'No vulgarity, no ugliness, no stupidity.' Lucy-as-nun ticks the rules off on her fingers. 'And finally you must swear not to get sidetracked by hormones, false promises and immoral behaviour, and never to just do whatever with whoever comes along at the time.' Lucy throws a bucket of ice water over Natasha's head. An ice cube bounces off Natasha's noise. It barely registers with Natasha. She wipes water from her face, but her expression doesn't change.

'Pray for me, Sister,' she says, water dripping onto the floor.

'I will pray that you turn into a magnificent young woman in a place that doesn't have time for the second rate. One final thing,' Lucy-as-nun says, 'you're going to need this.' She dumps the second bucket over Natasha's head, sending paper money flying through the air, the sheets settling onto Natasha's hair and soaking wet uniform.

'Thank you, Sister,' Natasha says and stands up. 'All of this has been very useful.'

Lucy blesses herself. Out of her robe, she pulls a toy gun. She slips off her nun-costume and underneath wears a stripy T-shirt and jeans. She grabs Natasha's hand. She shoots her toy gun into the ceiling. It emits a gentle flare. 'This is a stick-up,' Lucy shouts.

Natasha giggles nervously.

'We've got a girl here … '

'Me,' Natasha says.

'Who has been accepted to the best college in this country.' Lucy turns the gun to the front row, directly at the acting troupe. 'So you're going to need to put the money in the bag. We can't have her mucking around up there like a child from an uncultured and ugly hick town. Take a look around you, she's a long way from home. So let's get on with it.' She fires the gun two more times and, as she does so, Natasha and her separate. Natasha pulls the string and the screen fills the background once more. She puts a phone on the desk. She takes off her wet jumper and sits down. She wipes her face. She puts on Lucy's abandoned spectacles. Lucy drags in her own chair and sits opposite Natasha.

'It's so great to have you at this college,' Natasha says, 'and, as you know, we like to mind our students. So, Lucy, we're going to help you find your parents.' Natasha leans over and grabs Lucy's arm. 'We do this because we care. Lucy, are these your parents?'

Onscreen appears a picture of an elderly man and woman standing in a field of corn.

'No,' Lucy says.

Natasha nods in deep consideration. 'Lucy,' she says, seriously, 'are these your parents?'

A still from the film *Man of Aran* pops up. A black-and-white man and a woman standing in front of a sunken ship.

'No,' Lucy says, baffled.

The phone rings. 'Excuse me. I have to answer this but so help me God we're going to do everything in our power to find your parents, Lucy.' Into the phone, Natasha shouts: 'I don't care, get her down off that building. That would be the fourth this year. Get her down.' She slams the phone down. 'Hahahahah,' she laughs falsely, 'just a bit of business there. So where was the last place you saw your parents? Was it outside your shack?'

'My what?'

Natasha looks tortured. 'It's terrible. So terrible. A lot of the country girls come up here – they don't even have running water and electricity in their homes.'

'I don't think that's true,' Lucy says.

'We try to do what we can for them. We give them these little boxes at Christmas, it's just a little something, a token, but it helps.' The phone rings again. 'Excuse me,' Natasha says, and answers. 'She did WHAT? Why would she do that? That's dreadful. That's just dreadful. Clean it up.' Natasha hangs up. 'Well,' she says, 'we've lost another potential alumna. So, Lucy, tell me more about you. How did you find out about this college? You and your eighteen siblings were gathered around the television set and you saw a picture of it onscreen. Your heart was set on it.'

'That wasn't it.'

'That's actually a moving and beautiful story. We should put it in the newsletter.'

'But I—'

'So when the time comes and you've been out in the world for a while, we will be asking you for a donation to our establishment. Do you think you will be able to contribute?'

'I think you've got me all wrong,' Lucy says. 'Wait.' She walks offstage.

Natasha sits looking at the phone as if daring it to ring again. Lucy returns wearing everything she has ever stolen and been gifted. She can't be seen, her face and body are obscured by the pile of clothes and jewellery. She can barely walk. She clears a space in which only her mouth appears.

'Do I look like a lowlife to you?' she asks.

'You look good,' Natasha says. 'You look very good. But you're annoying me now. You're annoying me. Can we have some fun? I want to have some fun.' Out of the desk drawer, Natasha takes a sign that reads: 'Saturday Night.' She holds it up for the audience to see. Lucy waddles offstage. Natasha smoothes down a white tablecloth over the desk and places a vase of flowers on it. She also sets down a silver bell. She bows and exits.

Lucy swans back in, wearing her pink negligee and see-through robe. It is dirtier, more worn. She staggers in her heels and carries a comically tiny purse. She pulls out a chair and sits down.

She sits for two minutes before she shouts, 'What is taking so long?'

Natasha enters wearing a suit and a moustache. She sits down opposite Lucy.

'Why don't you eat something?' Natasha says to Lucy. 'You look so good but why don't you eat something?'

Lucy presses the bell. 'Next!'

Natasha changes quickly into a looser costume; a huge, white shirt.

'I have a poetic soul, you see.'

Lucy presses the bell. 'Next!'

'It was a transformative experience.'

Lucy presses the bell. 'Next!'

'Next!'

'Next!'

'Next!'

The bell rings out again and again as Natasha scrambles to change costumes faster and faster. She sways left and right as she pulls trousers and shirts on and off. She becomes more and more frantic until she collapses, lying motionless on the floor. Lucy just looks at her. Natasha stands up and calmly dusts herself off. She exits stage left.

Lucy is left alone at the table. 'Intimacy is hard for me,' she says, 'but I think I speak for all of us when I say it's hard for all of us.'

Natasha returns dressed in a coat and tails. She pulls a drinks cabinet behind her. She polishes a glass and places it in Lucy's waiting hand. She opens a bottle.

'How was your evening, Miss?'

'It was alright.'

'You tell me when now, Miss.'

Lucy holds out her glass and Natasha fills it to the top. When it begins to overflow, Natasha keeps pouring. She opens a second bottle and continues pouring until the liquid is all over the floor, all over the tablecloth and all over Lucy. Lucy stares straight ahead.

'When,' Lucy says.

Natasha takes a grey wig and waistcoat from the drinks cabinet and places it on the table. She pushes her drinks cart offstage left.

'What could be possibly worse than this on a Saturday night?' Lucy asks the audience. 'This set-up. You know I've thought some pretty distasteful stuff in my life, and actually done worse, but I don't deserve this. I'm generous. I try. What could possibly be more awful than this?'

From the other side of the stage, Natasha carries in a small table and a newspaper. She sits at the table. She is wearing a prim cardigan and a long skirt. Gentle, refined music begins to play. Lucy carries over her chair. She puts on the grey wig and the waistcoat. She picks up the newspaper and sits down, clearing her throat. She opens the newspaper. Lucy and Natasha sit in total silence as the refined music continues to play.

'What music is this?' Natasha asks.

Lucy raises one finger to silence her. She keeps reading the newspaper.

'What are you doing this weekend?'

Lucy raises a finger to silence her.

'What are you doing this weekend?'

A finger is raised again.

'What are you doing this weekend?' Natasha asks again, more quietly this time.

Lucy lays down her newspaper. She looks aggrieved. 'Why do you come into my house and ask what I'm doing this weekend, Natasha. I'm not your boyfriend.'

'What are you doing this weekend?' Natasha repeats.

A photo pops up onscreen: a blurry Lucy, her breasts on show.

'I'm working on my marriage,' Lucy-in-the-wig says, and picks up the paper again.

The lights go down to complete darkness. Lucy and Natasha switch costumes. They sit back down at the table where Lucy places a lamp and a tape recorder. The light from the lamp is all that illuminates the stage. Natasha switches on the tape recorder.

'So, Lucy tell me what happened?' Natasha says, business-like.

'I—' Lucy struggles.

Behind Lucy every photo she has ever taken flashes up on the screen in fast succession, a long parade of images. Lucy's hands clutching her breasts, spreading her legs apart.

Natasha watches the screen for a while. 'That's a problem,' she exhales slowly, in the manner of a weary detective. 'That's a problem, for sure.'

'What?' Lucy doesn't turn her head.

'We've got ourselves a slapper,' Natasha says. 'You know you should leave a polite amount to the imagination. Wipe that make-up off your gob. Stress your innocence, but not loudly, because that makes people suspicious. This is tricky. Don't be caught anywhere you shouldn't be. Spend a lot of time in the library. There are a lot of books in the library you can look at. Don't linger near any of the sexual stuff. Lead a normal, daily life. Be seen living a normal, daily life. Ride a bicycle. That's a good, carefree way of getting around. You trust a woman on a bicycle. That's essential, the bicycle. Try not to think about any pain. Are you paying attention? These things matter. Don't reply to any messages. Don't even think about replying to any messages. Don't get up in the middle of the night and send recriminatory and accusatory emails. Nothing good will come from that. Bury yourself, but at the same time be reborn. They will find your worst insecurities and they will kill you with them, so don't have any insecurities. Look after your family. Love all animals. Be respectful. Be seen to be respectful. Make some fairy cakes. This is image reha-bilitation. Take a good, long look at yourself. Not here, but in another building, away from me. Spend time in the garden. Reconnect. Change in every way, but don't be seen to be doing so. Do you have any questions? Are you tired?' Natasha turns off the tape recorder. 'I think once a few things are straightened out, we're in with a good chance of winning this thing.'

Lucy sits staring at her hands. 'Okay.'

'You can go now, Lucy.'

Lucy stands up to leave. She wanders, dazed, stage left.

'That's not the exit,' Natasha says, 'that's the exit.' She points the other way.

'Right,' Lucy says but stands still.

A set moves in on wheels. It's painted like a waiting room. In its confined space are two nailed-down chairs, a table with some magazines and a clock with its hands spinning frantically: day to night, day to night. In the corner is a large potted plant. Lucy and Natasha sit on the chairs. Natasha smoothly removes her grey wig and waistcoat, shaking out her hair. Elevator music blasts out – dull, non-distinct sounds.

'We're not allowed make a single joke here,' Natasha says.

'But—' Lucy says.

'No.'

'What if I—'

'No.'

'What do we then?'

'We wait,' Natasha says.

The girls sit in silence, leafing through their magazines, occasionally sighing, glancing at the distorted clock, examining their fingernails.

'I'm finished,' Natasha says, after five minutes. 'Goodbye.' She retrieves a massive suitcase from under the table. Natasha casually picks up the plant and starts bashing the suitcase with it. Lucy doesn't blink or move. She keeps flicking through the magazine, pausing on certain pages of interest. Natasha pounds the suitcase furiously, breathing loudly in and out with exertion. Lucy stands up and puts down her magazine. She stretches and walks off. Natasha wheels the set off. Natasha comes back in and removes the table. She pulls up the screen. For the first time, the stage is completely bare.

Lucy enters. She is dancing sloppily. She is back in her nylon bikini and is barefoot. 'I'm on holidays,' she announces to the audience. A fake sun is lowered from the ceiling, a happy face drawn on it. Lucy touches it gently. A phone is lowered from the ceiling, moving down inch by inch. Lucy pulls on the receiver.

'Stay on the line. Stay on the line,' she says, 'I'm not going to say anything mean.' She pauses, as if gathering herself. 'I just want to tell you that it's not just one thing. I nearly became a person who thought that way, but it's not. Many people don't know that and you're one of them.'

Lucy watches as the receiver is raised back up. She stands there for a moment before Natasha slides onstage in a similar bikini. She takes Lucy's hand.

'What would you like to do?' she asks. 'We can do anything you like.'

'Something dumb,' Lucy says.

The lights go down, completely black, and when they lift back up, Lucy and Natasha are sitting in a glass box. Lucy is retching into a bucket. Natasha sits on the floor beside her, holding her hair back. Lucy's phone rings and she lifts her head briefly to say, 'Tell him to fuck off, would you?' She continues throwing up.

Natasha takes the phone from Lucy's hand. She looks at it. She hesitates. She looks at it again. It continues to ring. 'Fuck off,' she says, quite kindly, into the receiver.

Lucy lifts her head up fully. 'I didn't think you would actually do that.'

'I'm getting brave,' Natasha says.

Lucy laughs. She rests her head on Natasha's shoulder. She closes her eyes. Natasha lifts the slab of glass from above their heads, and stars fill the glass box until it becomes a shimmering box of light. They stay inside for a few minutes before Natasha steps out and pulls the box offstage with Lucy remaining inside.

Natasha comes back out with the small table under her arm. She spreads out the tablecloth again. She retrieves two chairs and sets them down. She runs back and gets two cups and an afternoon tea set. She considers the table for a minute, before she sits down.

Lucy enters with a flourish. She is wearing a fur coat.

'Natasha,' Lucy says. 'It's me, your mother. I've been away but I'm back now. We can do anything you like. What would you like to do?'

Natasha gestures at the table. 'Just have lunch,' she says.

Lucy joins her and they clink teacups. They eat little pieces of cake from the set. Their conversation can't be heard by the audience.

As Lucy and Natasha talk, congratulating themselves in low voices, but saying goodbye too, the stage boy moves quietly around them. He is setting up a living-room space. The decor is drab, the wallpaper is ugly and old-fashioned, the lighting is low. He drags on a brown, battered couch and places a television with an aerial in the middle of the room. Lucy and Natasha move into the living-room space. They settle themselves onto the couch. Their faces glow in the blue of the television. Natasha pulls a string and 'Abortion, A Love Story,' spelt out in big letters falls over the scene. They sit and watch the television for a few minutes, both of them laughing.

'I'm not sure,' Lucy says. 'I'm not sure. I don't know if I get it.'

The light eventually fades on both girls.
Silence.
Blackout.
Curtain falls.

Track

My boyfriend, the comedian, took pleasure in telling me about rejection – how it came about, how to cope with in a dignified way, how it had dangerous, possibly cancerous elements. He claimed the link between cancer and repeated failure was irrefutable. He had a lot of unusual ideas. 'Feel that,' he said, grasping at my hips and thighs, 'that's the texture of rejection right there.'

My boyfriend was famous and I wasn't. When I walked down our tree-lined street in the city, I came back with styrofoam cups of coffee, croissants, souvenirs I considered mailing back to friends. When he walked down the street he returned aggrieved and frustrated by how much people adored him. He sent me out a lot. 'Get my coffee extra-hot,' he told me, like I was an assistant. 'I want it so hot it feels like hell,' I instructed the barista.

I loved my boyfriend. Our back and forth reminded me of black-and-white films I hadn't seen. Physically, we were unmatched. On forms, we were in different age brackets: he ticked one box, I ticked another. But we weren't the sort of people who filled out forms. He could get worked up about stuff he read on the internet and I knew how to make him happy.

'Here,' I said, handing him a snow globe containing a miniature Empire State Building, 'this is for you.'

'You're very sweet,' he told me. I guess it was true – I could be sweet. I was Irish. I didn't want to rely on it too heavily, do that whole bit, degrade myself. When my mother finalised the divorce from my father all she said was, 'Never give people what they want.' It was such good advice.

At the party, where I first met him, I explained that I wasn't a famous person and I had zero intention of becoming one. I wanted to make him laugh. I liked him. That didn't happen to me every day. 'Really,' I said, 'I nurse quiet neurotic suspicions that even the people who know me don't want to know me. That's the opposite of being famous.'

A week later, he moved me in. That first night, after I unpacked, I watched a topless man in the building opposite throw shirts out of his window. They were well-made, had seen fine interiors. I could tell by the way they flew. A rich, stiff quality that sailed nicely. The shirts fluttered, then fell, and slashes of green and pink stunned the sky. The man smiled directly at me as they hit the ground.

*

During our first few weeks together, he encouraged me to act. I looked like something audiences might want.

I didn't have a problem with the parts, but it was the rooms I had to go into to get the parts. It was the places I had to stand to get the parts. Before I walked in, I told myself, 'Get it right, get it right,' and then I froze.

Appraising women wasn't done anymore so it was all performed through a slippery new language I couldn't bear. Although I lacked presence, the directors appreciated the completely vacant thing I had going on. They said I was like a person vacuum-packed, sucked in tight, motionless. My boyfriend compared me to a painting of a glowing, alien foetus he had once seen – powerful but unborn. Same kind of look. Work that, he suggested. Own it. I nodded like I understood and I stopped auditioning.

Apart from acting I had my occasional job which was layering make-up on collapsing faces. I'd been improving faces for years, presenting my own as aspiration. I turned up to houses wielding my toolkit, scraped off undesirable features and pencilled in better ones. These women gave me advice for the city—find people you can trust, guard your skin against pollution, look both ways when you cross the street. But I didn't work much. I didn't have to. The comedian gifted me a roll of cash and I strolled around pretending I was invested in life's little things. It was summer and I sat in Broadway shows for the air conditioning, supped Diet Cokes and watched stage children slam doors, throw cute temper tantrums.

I ate bad food, food that wasn't immediately decipherable as food. You had to look at it for a while. I examined elderly women's ankles – puffy, tracked by large blue veins – on the subway. I looked forward to having ankles like this. It would make me sturdy and sturdiness was a state I always struggled to attain.

I knew if I spoke on the phone to my mother she would ask how I was doing and I would lie easily. In Ireland, my early twenties hadn't been kind to me and I'd had what I generously termed a 'restless period'. I'd started thinking it might be best if I was out of the way – but I wasn't sure what exactly I was standing in front of. There had been a grave and embarrassing incident involving an ambulance, my mother at my hospital bedside, tear-stained and suddenly worn, with an expression that just said, 'Don't dare put me through this again.'

At the recovery sessions, where I feigned boredom, the other depressives weren't friendly, as if they didn't quite take me seriously, implying that I hadn't, for reasons possibly to do with youth and make-up, earned my place there. Honestly, it felt as though I had shown up at a party to which I wasn't strictly invited. When I was no longer considered a risk to myself, I left. A nervous flier, I took pills on the plane. For three months, I slept on mattresses in trembling apartments, swayed by the subway. Then I met the comedian and my life became one impossibly smooth flight.

I liked our evenings together. I did small, bouncy things around the apartment, swept and wiped surfaces. I had nowhere else to be, no friends to visit, no family in the city. I took long, misty showers. I had full girlfriend privileges and a choice of soft, colourful towels. He told me he loved my face, the way it nodded and reassured. He didn't ask many questions about my life. He had strange, poverty-stricken ideas about Ireland, which he had caught from a regretful documentary, and referred to it only as 'that place'.

At night, he spent a lot of time on the phone speaking about his television show in low, nervous tones. He was older now, not as original or celebrated, and under his skin his organs seemed to swell outwards from stress. He was sort of a mild joke, but I was the one sleeping with him so I guess the joke was on me. Still, what's there to say about that early time? Nothing much. We watched television in bed, mooched around the apartment, lived in our own mess. They were some of the happiest months of my whole life.

*

But we started going out. That's where we went wrong. Once summer ended, we got dressed up and went out. That first night, before it all became usual, we went somewhere monstrous and glassy, a carpet rolled out like a plush red tongue. Atmospherically, this restaurant was not unlike a morgue in its coldness and we sat solemnly at a round table as if preparing for a seance. My boyfriend was seated far away from me, almost on a different continent, and he glanced over occasionally to see if I was still upright. He loves me, I thought. I examined the cutlery, my reflection in the cutlery, everyone's reflection in the cutlery. They were so easy to agree with, these well-dressed people! I had a thrilling, weightless feeling as if I had taken several painkillers. I remembered that I had taken several painkillers. I understood everything.

A woman appeared to me through a fog. 'So what was it like growing up where you came from?' she asked. 'Was it hard?'

I had no idea. All my memories were flat-green, postcard shaped. My parents, after their less than tender separation, became cartoon parents – fingers wagging into the frame of my life. When I told my friends I was leaving, they said it would be amazing. New York. So amazing. My hometown was a strange place dressed up as a normal place; it was as if we all lived under a sheet of suffocating plastic. I remembered my fingers trailing rental Debs dresses, the rubberiness of the dry-clean casing.

'Not many opportunities,' I said, 'for growth.'

The woman shook her head as if expressing incommunicable pain on my behalf. I smiled. I knew that smile would be the high-peak of my enthusiasm for the evening and I would awake in the morning, not as nicely drugged, with a new hate in my heart.

That rain-soaked night was the first time we listened to the track. When we returned to the apartment, he produced it as if he was doing me a favour. The track – its black tentacles coiling around two circular empty eye-sockets, trapped forever in a seventies style playback box – was his lucky talisman. A childhood gift from his mother, it was how he learned to hone his routine in the basement of his suburban home, pantomiming for an imaginary audience.

His mother was sick and growing up there hadn't been much joy in his house. He pressed play and manic laughter burst from the lips of the ancient tape. 'My mother was mentally ill,' he repeated as though he was strangely proud of it, as if it legitimised him. I could have tossed out some scraped-together psychology about his present situation, but what would it have been worth?

I imagined the comedian as a child, pirouetting desperately through his act, loosening an imaginary adult tie, preparing for a lifetime of being loved. A twelve-year-old channelling his frantic and obsessive energy in the basement, as the laughter drowned out the sounds from the other world directly above him. When I pictured his parents, I just saw them in regulation smocks, tilling the land, unsmiling.

He promised me I was the first woman he had shown the track to. He had dated lots of girls during his time in New York – some famous, some not, asymmetrical haircuts, cool and indifferent as if it were a career requirement. He liked to make mean, primitive remarks about his exes. It didn't bother me hugely. Types. The way he said types. I knew that a relationship could fall apart in the utterance of a single word, but this was not our word.

I didn't blame him. I was out there, stumbling around too. I was part of the show. Yet, that first night, when he dropped to his knees and thanked the track for his good fortune and success, I was oddly thrilled. He was a very neat person, tidy and composed, so this display of weakness was rare. As he paced through the bedroom – energetically rubbing his face, the laughter rising and falling, water leaking onto his cheeks like a reflex – I made encouraging sounds. I massaged his back, clockwise and anti-clockwise, watched him like an interested viewer. Afterwards, calmed by the noise, he felt moved to explain the different forms of comedy to me, working energetically through its history. At that moment, I have to say this – my chest grew extraordinarily tight and I felt it was very likely that I was going to die.

*

Over the next few months, the pattern continued – we lay in bed until evening, watched old comedies, listened to the track, had lazy sex. Then we got dressed up and went out. At the wide, marble dinner tables I was some combination of waitress and adoptee from a vague Third World country. I couldn't comprehend the performance that was required from me by him and his friends, most of whom were on television or hovering near it.

There was an older man at these tables, a man my boyfriend often referred to as his best friend, who was as wordless as I was. I happily misinterpreted his glances in my direction as solidarity. I was probably a bit high, finding meaning in nothing. My boyfriend often cracked jokes at this man's expense – about his comparative lack of success, his poor real-estate investments – and he remained motionless, his expression expired, taking it easily. I sat completely stationary as if that alone would help me evade humiliation. The man sometimes raised his glass towards mine in mute toast.

One afternoon, the comedian sent me out to the hairdressers before dinner. The salon was full of tanned women who picked over my scalp and commented on my blessed position. They gifted me a glass of champagne and I blew childish ripples in the surface. I left in the middle of the hair operation. I looked at my half-do in the mirror and said, 'Wow! That looks great. Thank you, thank you so much,' and I walked out. I expected security or someone like security to stop me at the door, but they didn't.

I spent the rest of the day wandering up and down the shaded, immaculate street my boyfriend and I called home. I wanted to make a discovery so I could feel like I lived there. At one end, near the subway station, was a psychic's office. She sat in a sturdy, high-backed chair and, apart from draping a red velvet curtain across the room to separate her office from her living quarters, did nothing to make herself look mystical. That's brazen, I thought as I passed. Only someone gifted would do so little to announce themselves.

That night, at dinner, nobody criticised my unusual hairstyle. It must have been decided it couldn't be an accident because nothing about the comedian was accidental. They gazed deep into my eyes and told me I looked great. When we returned from our excursion the comedian and I fucked coldly, like we were two expensive, shiny products, as if I was something sleek he could press that would produce the correct answers.

Afterwards, as we lay in bed, he asked, 'What do you want more than anything?'

'To be loved,' I said, just like that. Lately, I had become weary of the whole act I'd been cultivating. It was pathetic. 'You know, in Ireland,' I said, 'I wasn't well.'

Day to day he let me pretend to be whoever I wanted to be, a singular kindness. He had several versions of his own past; all that remained consistent was how he had overcome. In every version was the track and his mother staring blank-eyed beyond him into space. If he recognised any similarities between us, he didn't acknowledge them. I realised I didn't really know how this went. I hadn't had many boyfriends. Most of the boys I knew at home were terrified of me, though if I slept with them, they were briefly satisfied. I remembered the boy I was seeing when it happened, carting me around as if I was on loan, glamorous but refundable.

'Has that gone away now?' my boyfriend asked.

He wasn't dumb but he was coddled. He was like a man with a thousand relentless wives. He had people who designed his food, sourced his conversational material. They cut up his food, cut up his words. All that was left to do was open his mouth wide.

'Maybe,' I replied. 'I think I'm scared of death.'

'Depth?'

I considered. 'Both.'

We listened to the track together until dawn – the curtains closed, the darkness making our bodies indistinguishable shapes. It felt like intimacy, or as close to intimacy as we could get. The track had a sedative effect on him, steering him out of his manic period. I ran my fingers through his hair, soothed him, promised it was normal, that anyone would do it if they had the equipment. This was what he wanted more than anything, more than sex, more than love – to be told he was normal, to feel normal. As the sun came up, he encouraged me to read aloud online comments about him, bizarre and unflattering posts that implied he was past it. While I recited he looked bemused, like he was hearing outlandish conspiracy theories. At eight in the morning, I whispered him to sleep, kissed his eyelids. It wasn't something I would usually do. It was a gesture I didn't know I was capable of. In Ireland I would have dismissed it as sentimental but here, like entire days of solitude, dinners of pressed juice, it seemed fitting.

As the day his show returned closed in, he became increasingly agitated and his insomnia worsened. I didn't sleep well either and we wandered the apartment separately, moving in and out of rooms, ignoring each other like strangers. When I was sure he was asleep I got up and had a glass of terrible wine, wine that redeemed itself only by being alcoholic. I told myself I was okay, the best okay I'd ever been, but it was hard to believe it any more.

*

The night his show aired I got dressed up as I normally did. Even getting dressed had become a source of confusion for me. The comedian told me to display my body but that felt wrong to me – some small-town hangover. I wore an impersonal costume. I felt like I had ordered myself from a store window.

The dinner table rang with ugly laughter. My boyfriend was in public form. The desperation darted across his face, clawed up his cheeks. It was him but it wasn't. It was like walking into your house after it has been discreetly burgled. To his left was a young man in his early thirties, who talked constantly about wanting to learn a new language. Everyone at the table agreed that this was an excellent idea, self-betterment, refusing to allow dust into the brain.

'Get a foreign girlfriend,' my boyfriend advised, 'that's the only way you'll learn.'

'What language are you learning from her?'

This was something that happened. They discussed me in front of me. I looked the other way, pretended to be obsessed with the tablecloth.

'Poverty,' my boyfriend smirked.

He went easy on me – I sensed that others had suffered more – but this wasn't for my benefit. He was maybe scared he might disturb some beloved image of him I might have preserved from my girlhood when he was at the height of his fame. In truth, there was nothing – just a single blurry scene of him falling over, an amalgamation of gurning expressions. When we got back to the apartment, he watched the episode alone as if to punish me for some imagined slight. I wanted to apologise but I couldn't physically say the word, 'Sorry.' I hadn't slept in days.

When he locked himself in his bedroom, looping the laughter over and over, I logged onto the forum that followed my boyfriend's career. I scrolled through early, stand-up photos of him – long-haired, pretend bashful – accompanied by his most caustic one-liners, scrawled across the screen. Before I noticed my fingers moving, before I recognised the words, I'd left a detailed post where I declared the comedian not funny, suggested that he had never been funny and that hopefully, God willing, his show would be cancelled and he wouldn't inflict himself on us any more. I drew attention to his deteriorating appearance. I might have made a remark about his mental capabilities, which was out of character for me. I posted the diatribe under his mother's name and took two sleeping tablets. I passed out on the couch then, soothed by my own ugliness.

In the morning, after scouring reviews of his show, disturbed, he read the post back to me.

'Unbelievable.'

I made my eyes wide, saint-like.

'An extremely difficult person.'

'A sicko,' he said. 'Issues.'

'Oh for sure,' I agreed. 'Many issues. No doubt.'

*

Only once did the comedian notice my reticence at these gatherings. While his friends spoke about shows – who was on what show, the ratings of that show, a seemingly endless amount of shows – I enjoyed fantasies of being at the airport, walking uninterrupted through the departure gates, browsing through the duty-free, doing various breathing exercises at the carousel, watching a beautiful tide of bags tumbling out. They weren't imaginative visions. They wouldn't have received high ratings on any network. Still, it was impressive what was going on in my head – my own personal airport reality experience, complete with a one-way ticket.

'You're an odd little ghost person,' the comedian said, confrontationally, in the cab on the way home. It was late autumn and we'd been together for five months. I'd been feeling the sharp deterioration of our love for some time. I wasn't helping by staying up all night, leaving long, anonymous messages on the forum that hated my boyfriend. I'd established a lot of friendships on there, made meaningful connections. There were some nice people.

'I don't know what you're talking about,' I replied.

'Every dinner you don't say a word.'

'I say it all with my eyes.'

'Tell me one opinion you have.'

We fell into silence.

Back at the apartment he listed out the systems he'd organised so he wouldn't be able to listen to the track. Then he locked himself in the bathroom, ran the taps and listened to the track.

I knew he'd been talking to other women online. Deleting his browser history was something he just wasn't interested in. To pass the time, I rummaged through his clothes. He had them delivered from a company that dressed the modern man. It was all decided by filling out an oblique questionnaire about your childhood, when you lost your illusions, et cetera. He tried to get me into it. 'How was your childhood?' 'Not good,' I scrawled and handed the questionnaire back to him. He said I didn't deserve clothes and he was probably correct.

In the wardrobe I found his favourite coat and slipped in a printout of the most horrific post on the forum. I also included my fortune from the fortune cookies we had eaten earlier. I guess I still wanted us to have open communication. I couldn't let go. I could never let go. I didn't know how. A part of me was disgusted by how he treated me and another part was profoundly grateful.

Every day, there were two versions of me. The one who stayed and watched him with other women, leaning in, laughing – and then afterwards in cabs: listening to him object, argue, tell me I was a lot of work, a lot of hard fucking work. The me who had dreams where I climbed high, took a single breath and hit the ground like a shirt made of the cheapest, thinnest material. Then the other me – walking fast, with purpose, down the shaded street.

*

It was a cold winter and I stayed inside the apartment most days. I did my make-up and observed myself in the mirror, fearfully, as if I was an animal capable of bizarre and impulsive movements. I practised my accents so the neighbours would think there was a flurry of people who lived next door, a cultural mix, instead of just a comedian's girlfriend. I started watching the show, which, to my boyfriend's fury, had been moved to a daytime slot. Onscreen he played a professor – his waistcoat ill-buttoned, his face clouded with grief for the modern world, all his actions, romantic or otherwise, hilarious and large-hearted. The dialogue was bad and it bothered me to hear him say those lines. I felt implicated in a way, like a woman who sends her husband to war without even a kind word.

My boyfriend was king of a small and ineffectual country. He gestured to the scenery as if he had positioned it. If he questioned the morals of a character, in the next episode they would prove themselves to be loose, unworthy. When he pointed to the sky and said, 'Sure looks like snow!' snow fell immediately and coated the ground he stood on.

One afternoon, because of the painfulness of the show, I hid in the hall cupboard. I wanted to experience what it felt like to be closed away so I just climbed right in. It wasn't so bad in the cupboard. It was definitely the best place for me. The comedian had fired our permanent maid for what he claimed was 'sinister tampering with the track' so we had irregular replacements – trains of twenty-something women who trooped in and immediately out, distressed by the apartment.

We lived in immovable filth. It wasn't immovable exactly – we kicked it around – but we never completely rid ourselves of it. That day, the day of the cupboard hiding, the latest maid found me, swinging the door open and then shrugging her shoulders as if to say, 'Here we go, another rich wacko.' I didn't correct her. I didn't tell her I was poor with a decent personality, a fine personality, which I displayed to almost nobody. Her conviction that I was a wacko seemed to give her strength.

Before I came to the city, I'd never seen a maid. It wasn't something I grew up with. I imagined them all as fusty and evangelical, but this one was overweight, elderly and looked like she didn't give two true hoots about tidiness. I disliked the idea of her going through our things, hoisting out bags of our private rubbish, touching the spines of the empty books that lined the shelves.

I'm not a slow person but it took me several minutes of close monitoring to understand the connection between the maid and the street psychic. I recognised her faraway stare of other worldliness and her thick, veined ankles.

'You're not a maid,' I said, my hand thrusting in and out of a bag of Cheetos, 'you're a psychic.'

She just looked at me.

'Is it hard living a double life?'

I wanted her to say something supernatural like: 'You tell me,' or 'We all live double lives.'

There was a heavy sort of silence. 'Please rate me on the website,' she said, finally. That night, on the website, I picked the five-star option and gold stars flooded the screen one by one.

When my boyfriend returned I was seated in my usual place at the window, studying the opposite people, their dark and impossible lives.

'Did you have windows in that place?' he asked me cautiously.

'Not as clean,' I replied, smacking two fingers on the lower pane of glass. 'Smaller.'

The week after our encounter, I walked past the psychic's office at least twice a day. She looked sullenly ahead, chewing gum, flicking idly between cards, casually discarding fortunes on her foldable table. It was as if there had been no contact, no five-star review. She never once acknowledged me.

*

When we went out, I enjoyed the flickers of concern that passed over his rotating friends' faces. Should we know this one? I adjusted my skirt and watched incuriously, flatly, as my features blurred into the women before me. 'I'm new,' I said, like I was standing in front of a classroom. Those nights we monetised my normalcy until it became hard currency.

'She's so regular,' I heard him repeat, 'that's what I like about her.' So I said nothing about the week I spent on a ward unable to recognise my own face, a week when I felt it was possible I would never speak to another regular human being again. In every restaurant, they sat us right up front and if the comedian demanded snow, snow fell from the ceiling.

*

Over time, the stuff my boyfriend did became sort of predictable – staying out late, or not coming home, or coming home reeking of downtown places. If I'd ever once spoken on the phone to my mother, I know she would have referred to this as 'evidence'. She would have used the phrase 'cheap women'. Like anybody, she had phrases she used frequently. I wanted to ask him, 'Are you going to downtown places?' but I didn't exactly know where the downtown places were. They could have been downtown or they could have been uptown. They might have been in the middle. Then again, anywhere is seedy if you want it to be.

He also moved the track into our bedroom and forced me to sleep on the couch. He said it comforted him to hear the laughter at night. It improved his routine.

'What routine?' I asked.

'Sorry,' he said, piling up blankets and pillows.

I saw a doctor for my sleep problems. It was necessary. She shone a light under my tongue and performed other technicalities. A week later, I was informed I had several STDs, some of the minor ones, but also some of the major ones. I inquired whether I got them all at once, or at different times. The doctor said she couldn't tell, her education only went so far. She awarded me prescriptions and a lollipop.

When I asked my boyfriend about it, he just ignored me, made me shower twice a day, repeated the weak jokes he told his mother at her lowest. If I mentioned the track, how the laughter scared me at night, he whispered, 'We will not survive without that machine,' and closed his eyes tightly.

I felt an uncontrollable terror on that couch, as if my life were speeding away from me, slipping and sliding, like a visual gag. I drew a rough sketch of the apartment and mailed it back to my mother with a note that said, 'I'm very happy here.' In many ways, I missed her, her way of looking at the world. She would have referred to my stint on the couch as 'a little holiday'.

The evenings my boyfriend disappeared, I went to the pharmacy and picked up things. American things that made me happy: teeth-whitening strips, colourful candy, painkillers, sleeping tablets. On the street, not far from the psychic's office, was a store shaped like a large barn that had everything I needed. I spent shameful hours in the yellow light. The sight of a mustard bottle and a ketchup bottle side by side often moved me to tears. It seemed so wholly patriotic, like the flag that billowed from the comedian's fake university.

One quiet evening, as she scanned through my items, I spoke to the counter-girl. She was young and I wondered if she went to college, had a father who mocked her intelligence, a boyfriend who picked her up from work. I went on like this for a while before I said, 'I like this store.'

'It's okay.' She examined my tablets, eyeing the amount and dosage carefully. 'Are you taking a long and nervous journey?'

I thought of my walk from the television to the cupboard.

'Yes.'

She continued scanning. I looked at her.

'You probably want to be famous,' I said. 'All young girls do, but let me tell you, my boyfriend's famous and it's not worth a damn.'

She took in my tatty coat, my unwashed hair. People can be very critical with their eyes.

'He has some trouble on the internet,' I continued, 'it's nasty on there.'

Any space between us closed up.

'Who is he?'

I told her his name.

'Don't get excited,' I said. 'He listens to a laugh track at night, he's going very weird. He believes it keeps him funny. It's a fantasy. He's a fantasist.' I rolled my eyes in an exaggerated way. 'He has a lot of things wrong with him, deep in his soul. Have you ever met anyone like that? And I think he's sleeping with other women. You could be one of those women if you liked? I mean if that's something you wanted to do – sleep with some-one famous and tell your friends about it?'

She was quiet for a while. 'No thanks.'

'Cool,' I said. 'Thank you for your service.' I breezed into the open air with my plastic bag of new belongings. Out on the street I paused and thought: I will not be a person who abandons others. No, that's simply not me. I walked back into the store and confronted the counter-girl.

'Excuse me,' I said. 'Do you have anybody to walk you home? This is a dangerous neighbourhood.'

She looked up. 'This is probably the best, maybe second best, street in the entire city.'

'I see,' I said thoughtfully, considerate. 'I'm sorry. I really don't know where anything is.'

On my journey back I thought of that girl selling her story to the ravenous tabloids, getting a small bit of tawdry cash, taking her friends out for drinks, saying a few words in my honour. In the kitchen I unpacked and divided the tablets into ones I would take now, ones I would take later and ones I would take in a relaxation emergency.

I took the track out of the comedian's bedroom and examined it. I'd never been alone with it before. The laughter was a solid sound, the mirth of an old-time audience who meant it. I considered ripping its guts out and leaving the entrails on the kitchen table. I wanted to know how that would sit with me. But I didn't destroy anybody that evening. I turned off the track and slithered around on the couch for a while.

At two AM, the intercom buzzed. I wasn't sure what I expected. A soft comforting voice on the other end telling me not to be scared? Someone to have an emotional moment with? God himself? 'Hello,' I said. I recognised the breathy tones of the psychic immediately. And she told me everything that would happen to me. It wasn't terrible but it was empty. It was one long flash of emptiness. I shouldn't have been surprised. Over that intercom, into the early morning, the psychic and I lamented and cried and offered the sincerest condolences to my life.

*

Summer returned and I stood, naked, in front of my air conditioner, feeling expert bursts of air all over my body. I got the air conditioner for free from a guy on the forum who left a rambling message about how he was leaving the city. When I collected it, I pretended to be a regular woman with no connections to the comedian. Whenever I walked into an apartment – no matter the size or shape – I felt sad for all my losses, for everything I couldn't do.

He had a new girlfriend on the show. It had been a dull season and he needed someone to rub off. I watched her daily, peeking out warily from my place in the cupboard, drool pooling around my mouth, as if all the water wanted to leave my body. They tried to make her whole- some, a fellow professor, but she had certain aspects that couldn't be contained – her breasts, her lips. I figured she was from Miami or LA or one of those places, had seen a lot of ceilings. I wanted friends so I could imitate her, call her 'Candy'. Make myself feel good.

One afternoon, I came home and heard them having sex. It wasn't a secret. I was supposed to hear. I stood in the hallway and tried to guess the position. Afterwards, we went out. All three of us got dressed up and went out. In the cab, he told her she was the first person he'd played the track for. I went into the restaurant bathroom to throw up but found I couldn't. On the bathroom floor, I felt my whole body shrink, like it could fit in a suitcase, be placed on a baggage carousel.

At dinner I was seated beside an older, stately woman my boyfriend called his agent. He handed me over to her. She ran her eyes over Candy and me, said it was just beautiful to see girls who could carry themselves correctly. I wanted Candy to do something that confirmed my low expectations of her – flash teeth, simper – but she looked towards the door. I withdrew my hundred imaginary phone calls to my hundred imaginary friends.

The agent reminded me of the psychic. In a way I couldn't explain she was the psychic, completely her, so when she took my hand and said she would help me, I trusted her. She made me want to be a baby again, tiny and clean.

'Now,' she said, 'I bet you would like a part on the show?'

A week later, I stood on set, in the vast maze of the fake university, feeling the weight of a mop in my hand. On a hanger beside me was a maid costume wrapped in plastic. The costume was like a question to which I had no answer. I wondered how I would put it on. In the normal fashion, I presumed. I would put it over my head. Then my neck. But what would happen after that?

I stopped a woman who was having trouble with her headset. 'May I use the bathroom?' I asked quietly.

She nodded. But I didn't go to the bathroom.

I walked outside as if I was going home. But I didn't go to the apartment either. I kept walking, a lone figure crossing a city desert. I thought about all of the things I had forgotten about myself and I tried to remember. Soon I was on the subway and an older woman, with brown-spotted, delicate ankles appearing from under her skirt, like feelings I couldn't describe, smiled at me. I thought about my mother's face then and I tried to picture it. Then off the subway and into the light. And I thought I would like weather – thunder, lightning, snow. I thought I would like weather and snow came from the sky.

Parrot

When she thought about the second woman – and she had distantly when she'd been younger; how her life could potentially be upended by someone she didn't know – it was always with a sort of black amusement. And when she said things that were improper – lines about her current situation that were just slightly off, the dry delivery of which was the reason why her friends were her friends – she had to admit, if only to herself, that she never imagined she would be the second woman.

That afternoon, still within their first six months in Paris, she went to an art exhibition. Exhibitions were something she was trying out, attempting to adjust to their sophistication, their unique shush. She moved up and down the staircase, cheapening the place with the cut of her clothes, searching for her soul at a frantic pace that suggested she was rummaging through a demolition site for the remains of her belongings rather than spending a pleasant few hours in a museum. She was not alone. The boy was with her, suspended from school for the day, a fact to which he was largely indifferent. At only nine years old he had learned to handle disappointment and failure with the sort of grace that, in her early thirties, still escaped her. He set the tone for the afternoon, ignoring her under the pretence of looking at paintings of nondescript benches. In a corner of the exhibition, there was a cage with two stuffed parrots. The woman spent an unnatural amount of time staring at them. They seemed as if they had been there forever, loving and admiring each other. How could they leave? They were behind bars. Nobody knew what happened in the tiny parameters of their cage.

Recently, at a dinner party, with her husband's new colleagues she had – seized by the closeness of the couple, the sudden tininess of their Parisian apartment – explained that at home, in the Irish countryside, all of the houses were built far apart, with long driveways, so you could easily get away from your family. She did the smooth, fluid motion of a driveway with her hands.

'They are legally obliged to be that way,' she said.

Afterwards, she felt stupid, like she had revealed more than she intended. The woman half of the couple, wearing heavy, intimidating jewellery that implied intellectual heft, suggested that perhaps that was only in her family. Perhaps, she agreed. Therapy, she considered, as she flipped through the art books in the gift shop – their pages full of unnerving, confusing beauty – was also something new she could try.

As they walked back through the city streets, the October cold not wholly unpleasant, the boy sloped two steps behind her, but in her eyeline, always in her eyeline. As they strolled, history announcing itself at every corner, she answered a call from her mother. Since they had moved, her mother rang a lot and spoke in her usual steady stream, like she was being held hostage and needed to get all the information out before her throat was slit. The woman understood this way of speaking only after she became a mother herself. She would barely be recovered from one of these conversations when another would happen. Her mother was retired and bored. What was she supposed to do now? What was she supposed to do in that house? Just thinking about it made her want to get another job.

'Don't do that,' the woman said, 'start going to exhibitions. I've just been to one.'

'I thought you didn't like art.'

'I don't like artists. There's a difference.'

When she let herself and the boy into the apartment they were renting, all the apartments built discreetly into the architecture of the city as if to obscure the fact that families lived in them at all, there was a notice on the front door. It was a picture, not unlike those in the exhibition, but less celebrated, of two cockroaches, one on the left, one on the right, with X's running vertically through their bodies. There were some words promising there had been cockroaches and now they were gone, or there was an ongoing effort to get rid of the cockroaches.

She wasn't sure. She didn't read or speak French. Later, in bed, with her husband, under crisp, ironed sheets, she tried to sleep off the possibility of cockroaches.

'I love you,' he whispered.

She blinked anxiously in the dark, as if trying to identify something. 'Go easy on that stuff,' she advised him.

*

Maybe the problem was that she was tired. She had been a bit tired when she entered art college, but dropping out had exhausted her. She remembered the final meeting, her prepared speech about why she was leaving, the made-up family reasons; then interrupting herself; then, finally, silence.

'You should leave if you're unhappy,' they said.

'I'm unhappy because I don't think I belong here.'

Nobody begged her. It was cute that she had tried in the first place. She put the sculptures she had made in her first year in her parents' garage and her mother used them to hang up wet clothes.

This was a serious decision but she didn't know it until a few years later. She stayed in Dublin to work, sharing shabby rooms with a series of men. Through these relationships she wanted to prove something, prove that she was still complicated and interesting without a degree, but there was no time. She was too busy picking up after her boyfriends, making disappointed faces, listening to them complain about the inconsequences of their actions. She felt like a mother forcefully pushed on stage in a farce, with only an apron and a spatula. Why wouldn't they let her commit the delinquency she knew she was capable of? Why was she always standing next to the delinquents, apologetically shaking her head?

All these relationships ended the exact same way, with circuitous conversations and dully rational arguments, as if both participants were politicians lobbying for their own happiness. Denied even heartbreak and animosity, the modern emphasis was on the demonstration of respect, however insincere. In her last relationship, before she met her husband, he respected her so much he let her pay for everything. 'This is respectful,' she thought as she paid their rent, as her credit card hit the illuminated screen again and again. When he ended it, she felt like she had been mugged – robbed of money, but also of time.

'I still respect you,' he said.

'I don't care if you do or you don't.'

'But I do,' he said earnestly, 'I really do.'

She was so tired.

He moved his stuff out and she continued doing the scrambling necessary to staying alive; working two jobs in the city, her personality dissolving into small talk. The cost of travel, the cost of lunch, the cost of being young.

She met her husband in an office where she was a temp, the irony not lost on her, irony never lost on her. She treated these temp jobs like cocktail parties, draping her sparkling self across surfaces, trying to dazzle in a limited amount of time. He devastated her with the ease that he saw through her. He filed away her exaggerations, her evasions, the playfulness that was beginning to curdle into meanness so he could eventually embarrass her – a child in an adult place. When, one lunchtime, through a mouthful of sandwich, she laughed at a man in the office, because every office must have someone sad to laugh at, he frowned at her.

'That man is depressed.'

'How do you know that?' she asked.

'How do you not?'

She drafted an email where she declared it was up to her what she decided was funny. Instead, she offered to buy him a drink. She hadn't meant what she said. She explained, in careful email language, that she was beginning to suspect she might be a bad person. She had dropped out of college and there had been a number of other severe and deranged fuck-ups. Several weeks later, nudging, overly friendly correspondence passing between them daily, he kissed her for the first time, his hands touching the back of her neck.

They always went to the same B&B, the same room, fringed lamps and light curtains. It was like an affair made on an assembly line, everyone playing their part, following a strict pattern. No poetry, no sunlight on the bedsheets. The only surprise was when she found, unbelievably, like discovering a hidden room in a house, that she was in love with him.

They only had one discussion about his wife, and it barely qualified as a discussion. She was ill and had been for a long time. Her illness would never be over. He had done everything he could. She believed him, not because he was a man who could ever be accused of heartlessness, but because he looked like someone who had begged and cried and tried to reassemble and done everything he could.

*

The winter in Paris, two days before Halloween, grew harsh and the woman's lips cracked what felt like audibly. She was concerned strangers on the Metro could hear, as if her mouth were a strip of velcro to be peeled open and closed. She knew she should be worried about presentation, in a city that demanded presentation, but she sloughed the dead skin off, forced her teeth into the supple, comforting grooves. Smiling was the only communication available to her and, overnight, it had turned ugly. Still, she continued smiling, amiably, like a tourist, like a secretary, like a combination of both – a tourist's secretary.

She was called to the boy's school, English-speaking, private, already more than they could afford, at least once a week. She went because she wasn't working and for other, more defiant reasons. The school was a monstrous structure on a street of other dutiful buildings, including a police station, their insides deep and hidden. The boy had behavioural problems, concentration issues, the whole catalogue. She had humorous lines prepared about how they were more alike than they knew, how she might be his mother after all, but the teacher never gave her a single opportunity.

Every Monday or Friday, the woman sat in a child's chair and struggled for a position that lent her some dignity. She could offer nothing concrete – that his behaviour would improve or that she would insist it improve. Her presence there only promised she would be at the next meeting and the meeting after that, all the way to graduation and beyond. And although it made both her and the teacher uneasy in a way they couldn't articulate, she had to come in to prove her worth, her plans to stay.

He had been caught stealing from another boy's pockets.

'Maybe he was just curious about what was in the pockets. Curious,' she repeated, hopefully.

The teacher gave her a stern look, violently shrinking, and the woman wondered who educated these people, schooled them in disapproval. 'That wasn't it,' the teacher said. She was from London and had a soundless way of communicating disappointment. Their relationship never moved beyond professional; they never hinted at their personal lives, as if any friendliness might cause embarrassment the next time they saw each other, and there would be a next time.

The woman pulled a face that was also learned, perfected from years of bad relationships – let down but doubtful of change.

'I will speak to him,' she said, finally.

On the Metro, hurtling home through black tunnels, he sat beside her, always content in her company. He kept up a steady chatter about school as if constant talk could distract from his misdemeanour. She was familiar with this trick. If she ever tried to grab his hand, he shook her off. He never allowed her to touch him.

When she watched the other mothers exit through the school gates – in their discreet, mother uniforms; this city believed in uniforms – pushing their sons' hair back from their eyes, casually shepherding them, her mind raced with thoughts of self-improvement. She should try to be gentler, less agitated, learn to make small talk in another language, or even her own language. Become someone a boy might want to touch. It seemed as if her whole life, from the age of thirteen onwards, had been geared towards that rotten desire and now the world had come up with a genius way of punishing her.

She tried to tempt him into a pastry shop, bribe him into confessing with sugar. It was gloomy. It was also possibly criminal.

'No, thanks,' he said, massaging his abdomen, his body so tiny that it was hard to believe that it contained the correct amount of organs. 'Sports.'

'Sports.'

'Sports,' he repeated and raced ahead of her.

She considered, not for the first time, becoming one of those mothers who carries fruit with them everywhere, pulling it out of the insides of their handbags like a magic trick, eternally resourceful. On the front door, beside the cockroaches, although she tried not to look, tried not to be confronted with her own ignorance of the French language too often, was a notice with a photo of a rat, no X running through it, free to do what he pleased. It was a vicious rat, his tiny teeth bared. He looked motivated.

When the boy went to the bathroom, she flicked through his phone, the one concession they allowed him. There was never anything of concern, just a sadness attached to it, a lonely phone gasping for contact. She watched the clips he had recorded from the police station across the road from the school, his newest fascination. Blue-uniformed boys wandered blurrily back and forth, groups of two or three, trying to look busy or brave, or both. They were armed in a traumatised city, their hands resting on their guns as if the gesture alone could reassure what happened before would never happen again. There were only five clips, shaky and accompanied by the raucous playground laughter of boys, but she watched them to the end.

*

The first time his wife called the police the woman went to the station with her own mother. They drove in silence. In the reception, they sat side by side and her mother advised her to just be herself, as if that – the whole process of being herself – wasn't exactly why she was here in the first place. They waited in the exact same way, patiently, showing no hint of irritation, both betraying their own telltale signs of anxiety – her mother rummaged constantly in her handbag, the woman ran her fingers over greasy patches of her skin. A policewoman smiled gently at them, before beckoning the woman into a room. The woman remembered how she and her mother used to go to the bogs, weekend rebellions, the two of them running wild, comfortable in the dirt. Once, she slipped into a trench and had only managed to wade through the deep muck with her mother's careful encouragement. The walk from one side of the station to the other was like that.

In the small, airless room she was told they had received a phone call from his wife. Her car had allegedly been stolen and the woman was the prime suspect, the only suspect. The doubt was in the allegedly. She knew that a policewoman was being used for her sensitivity, and she wondered how many sensitive cases she had to handle a week, and how much sensitivity she had left.

The policewoman's shirt was untucked, her eyes heavily ringed, her shoulders drooped; all those crime-free hours spent at pedestrian crossings, waiting in cars, weighing on her, transforming her waistline. The woman thought she looked ridiculous. When the policewoman placed a hand over hers and declared it a domestic situation, her dislike didn't alleviate. There was no decency in the movement, only the desire to dominate.

'We can't throw you in jail,' she said, with a tight, mean smile, 'just for being a silly girl.'

'Why?' she asked. 'Not enough room?'

The policewoman scowled at her.

'I'm sorry,' she said. 'I'm so tired.'

On the way back, her mother pulled the car into a quiet stretch of motorway so she could cry freely, tears vandalising her face, emotion she didn't know she had left in her. Her mother let her cry, even allowed her to veer into self-pity, before she asked was she upset because the police didn't think she could rob a car. They laughed despite themselves, a dark hollow-sized trench hiding inside it, surprised they were still capable of making the sound.

The second time his wife reported a made-up crime, he went alone. He explained that after the birth of their son, his wife had developed postnatal depression, then just depression, the regular kind. So she can be difficult sometimes, the police said.

When he came home to the house they were now renting together outside Dublin – in an estate of identical houses so alike that she often arrived at the wrong door – the back of his work shirt was soaked, and he was shaken in his own unshakeable way. In the middle of the night, he woke up, his breath sour, and told her he didn't like the word difficult, had never liked it. They didn't smile then, they wouldn't dare, but there were still whispered jokes between them, in trouble with the law, like two teenagers on the lam.

The third time the police got involved in their lives, they went together. A teacher had discovered bruising on the boy's body, still and silent purple lakes, signs of abuse. After an investigation that moved slow, then fast, everything being worked out in rooms that didn't include them, the boy's mother was declared unfit and he was sent to live with them permanently. 'By who?' the woman wanted to ask, 'declared an unfit mother by who?' They had a few interactions with the same policewoman from her first encounter, the police seemingly attached to them now. She sometimes looked at the woman like she forgave her. This makes it easier for you. You must be happy now.

They married in an embarrassed ceremony shortly before they went to Paris. It was a year after the funeral; he changed suits. Her friends donned confused formalwear. She was having them on, right? No one could be this in love, no one could make this sacrifice. Certainly not her. They thought the production of her life, always entertaining, was never going to end. She spent a lot of time in the bathroom, avoided the food, searched for her mother's features in her own when they stood side by side in the mirror.

Throughout all of this, the boy said almost nothing and she watched him like he was a crucial witness. Everything she knew about him was mediated through others: his teacher, his father, the guards. He had to speak sometime though. That was the deal in this life – no matter how much you tried to avoid it, you had to speak sometime.

In bed with the man in the weeks before the ceremony – still her boyfriend then, fiancée if she felt like being technical, both terms startlingly trite for what they were trying to do – he held her tightly in his sleep as if she were going to sneak out. A restless one-night stand. His grief had been huge, paralysing, and the guilt was worse. So they put a ban on sadness, binned newspapers, left the television on cartoons of pink hyperactivity.

Grief had a time frame and when they reached the end of that time frame, and he wasn't recovered and neither was his son, money was the problem. If they had money, they could somehow circumnavigate the time frame. He was in numbers and was constantly trying to beat the morose odds, trying to outrun a train. He wanted to make her happy. It was her turn to be happy. People were the problem for a while, general people and then, more specifically, this country. This country was going to make him exercise, this country was going to make him get up early, this country was going to make him put a brave face on it. Let's go somewhere, he said, that makes miserable a look, that smiles only when it absolutely has to.

'Paris,' she said.

She bought a guidebook and flipped through it before bed. It was just pictures of macarons and rich, oppressive buildings. There was no guidance in it. At night, she curled her body into a promise in answer to his clawing question: she wouldn't leave them.

*

There was occasionally something so cheerfully immoral about the city that it caught her off guard, made her feel like her former self. Go and have an absurd love affair, it told her. Go on. You've done it before. Do it again. Walk around naked underneath your coat. She considered the possibility that everyone was naked underneath their coats. It wouldn't surprise her. The city was silent during the day and loud in the evenings, and the sudden transition alarmed her. It could be bossy in that way – be scared, don't be scared, now be terrified. Once the Metro came to a stop, the lights died, total silence, not even a cough. Then it moved as normal. There was the sense of an unspoken resilience. Every Monday or Friday, regardless of where she was, how unpredictable she was feeling, she received a phone call from the school. This was what she talked about when she rang home. In a city of novelties, responsibility was the only real novelty.

It was Halloween when she next stepped into the boy's school, passing by unremarked except for a few fake skeletons dangling from the ceiling, an unsophisticated holiday. When she stood in the hallway, feeling like a student herself, the place spoke to her of sweat and failure. Already, at under twelve, there were violin, piano, language lessons abandoned, a sluggishness set in. A sea of uniforms swept over her; a tide of blue. The boys all had bad posture and awkward gaits as if ashamed of their childhoods. Why are you so sluggish, she wanted to ask. Perk up. Many of you are going to be rich.

'What's the collective name for a group of boys?' she asked the teacher.

'In French or in English?'

'English.'

'I don't know in either language.'

'A school of boys, maybe,' the woman said, 'a drooping of boys.'

The teacher always so elegant, yet merciless, in her admissions, told her that morning the boy had hit a classmate – slapped him hard across the face for beating him at a race.

The woman was quiet for a moment. 'He doesn't get this from me.'

'No,' she said, delicately.

'I'm the stand-in.'

The teacher gave a curt nod in response.

She leaned forward awkwardly in her chair. 'You think I'm not trying.'

'I don't think that.'

'I love that boy.'

'I know you do.'

A silence passed.

'We don't want to have to expel him.'

'I will speak to him,' she said, 'I will speak to him.'

'He's very good at running,' the teacher said, a genuine smile on her face. 'Fast.'

'He does get that from me,' she said and closed the door.

In the hallway she waited for him, watched the overhead skeletons, seemingly relaxed without a skin. She spun one in her hand, made it dance. It seemed to resent the movement. A private school, she thought, its skeleton private.

On the way home they stopped at the playground beside an imposing church. The city constantly humbled her, reminding her at every opportunity that people had been there before, waving its hands around in excitement about its incredible history. It was irritating. Out of his schoolbag the boy took out a drawing of a ghost, the eyes far apart, in opposite hemispheres. Squiggles representing horror. She wasn't sure if he was proud of it.

'That's a beautiful picture,' she said, cautiously.

'No, it's not.'

'No,' she agreed, laughing, 'it's not.'

She sat on the wooden bench, her breath rippling out in stubborn, icy waves in front of her. She watched him climbing, tried to spot any trace of athletic talent. Then she watched for what she was told to watch for – any signs of trauma, an impulse toward sadness.

She never socialised with the other mothers. It was ridiculous, her attitude problem resurfacing. She felt they knew she had been coerced at the last minute, didn't have the correct paperwork. She had never held him as a baby, never heard him cry, a cooing from another world. She once listened to sounds of babies crying and decided which one he would have sounded most like. It was a high-pitched, argumentative wailing. She went on the websites with the mothers of newborns, introduced herself. There were some genuine points of interest but nothing to help with a nine year old.

'Are you a troublemaker?' she asked when he, out of breath, sat down.

'No.'

'That's what troublemakers say.' She rested her arm behind him. 'Tell me about running.'

'It's stupid.'

'I like stupid things.'

'You like stupid things?'

'Yeah, I like stupid things,' she said loudly, finding freedom in it. 'That's why they kicked me out of college.'

'You got *kicked out*?'

'I kicked myself out. But it was the same thing. Tell me.'

It was fun, he explained, it was good, but to be the best you had to keep practicing and what was the point? It was a version of the argument she had with herself daily. She wanted to encourage him but what was she supposed to do? Tell him, like a dog, to sit down, stand up, kneel? She had no authority. Why was she even here? What did she want from it all – a medal?

On the Metro, at the last stop, she asked him outright. 'Why did you hit that boy?'

'The medal,' he said simply.

On the front door she stuck the picture of the ghost and drew a large, deliberate X.

That night, in bed, her husband described his day and she listened. He was in love with the city, wandered around in a loving daze. The distance was good for him and, although his work was difficult, obscure, he was now a medium shade of grey, instead of a deep shade.

'How did you know it would be right?' he asked.

'I know everything.'

*

She had been to Paris once before with her mother when she was twenty, a few months after she dropped out and it didn't look like she was going back. She had settled into the rhythms of the joke but her mother knew, instinctively, without having to be told, how disappointed she was. It was a cheap trip; they shared a hotel room. Their room contained a tiny, electric Eiffel Tower.

They were women who knew dirt, country roads, had learned to make conversation in corner shops. Confronted, finally, by glamour, by seriousness, they did everything wrong. They went to the wrong bars, the wrong restaurants, the wrong streets. She wasn't sure they saw Paris at all, neither of them exactly clear on what a holiday was. They fought on several street corners, made up, and hid their giddy laughter behind their hands. The city was impatient with them. What is so funny, it asked. What could possibly be so funny? Her mother made her go to every museum and when her feet were sore she waited in the cafes. She remembered seeing her across the crowded room, her soles exposed, sitting patiently, waiting for her daughter, looking like an old woman.

'You will make a great old woman,' she told her mother that night.

'I am an old woman,' her mother said.

Later, in their twin beds, she asked her mother was she hard to raise.

'You had an answer for everything. Everything.'

'I don't anymore. Not at all.'

Then her mother, a shadow on the wall of the hotel room, told her that she regretted some of her life. The usual. She would have liked to do more, although she didn't really know what: live in European countries, make mistakes. She never had the time to figure out what it was. She felt her life was small, mechanical. She spoke for a while.

'I shouldn't have said all that,' she decided, after a thoughtful pause.

'It's okay,' the woman said, 'it's fine.'

'I had a nice time.'

'I had a nice time too.'

They fell asleep, after a while, Paris coming through the slats of the hotel blinds.

*

She only saw the boy's mother once. It was the woman's fault for recognising her, for being too thorough in her investigations, combing through photographs – looking for what exactly? Evidence that he had adored her, evidence that she had once been someone you could adore. It was in a hardware shop, the woman had gone to buy some paint. She wandered through the shop, marvelling at the anarchic presentation, broken pieces of domesticity everywhere, a sink just sitting in the middle of the floor. It was a joke shop, everything too large or ominous or numerous, hundreds of versions of the same thing, everything gesturing towards a great future. In the lighting section she turned a lamp on and off, imagined it on her bedside table, a matching one opposite, lamps came in pairs. She was decorating the house, no longer able to look at the white walls.

It was in the paint aisle, staring businesslike at the selection, that she felt the boy's mother. It occurred to her that they were both standing in front of a wall of paint and that if they had been two different women, they could have been standing in the glow of a painting, a scene that would at least lend some ceremony. But they weren't, and they weren't. The tins of paint stretched far back into the wall.

She glanced at the boy's mother sideways, but didn't fully look at her, because she knew then she would have to look at her twice, to see if she could tell from her face, from the planes of it, the missed medication and the locked cabinets and the attempts with the kitchen bleach. In exactly a week the boy's mother would be dead, succeeding at what she had been trying for a lot of her life.

The woman didn't turn her head. She looked fixedly ahead and felt the boy's mother only as a presence. She wanted to apologise, explain that she hated it all too, fake pleasantness and being alive and fucking paint, that nobody blamed her, but when she looked around, she was gone. It was like a dream and, afterwards, in the car, the paint on her lap, the light came through the windshield blindingly strong, like in a dream.

*

When she got a chance she went to cafes and pretended to be a tourist, a woman with a book and a coffee. That afternoon, underneath the coffee, she could smell the boy's laundry on her – the clothes she had washed and dried earlier. In the long mirror that wrapped around the cafe, she watched herself, not like her idea of a mother, but when she smiled, resolved to smile, the face that looked back was her own mother's. In the cafe, a parade of faces worked at their food and drink. A man walked around with a baby, clutching him to his chest.

Her husband's colleagues told her that after it first happened, you could see people quietly scanning the exits in bars and restaurants. How long would it take to escape? One minute? Two minutes? She waited for the call and, when it came, she went to the school. On the Metro she thought about how easy it would be to step off somewhere else, disappear. It occurred to her that, for the whole of her life, she might never stop having that thought.

'I haven't seen you in ages,' she said to the teacher.

'It was three days ago.'

'I know.'

'It was three days ago. I remember, believe me.' There was the flicker of a bold smile.

'I admire your relentless professionalism.'

'Thank you.'

She walked behind the teacher, following the clip-clop of her work heels through the long corridor of identical lockers. They walked up several flights of stairs, until they came to a door marked 'No Entry.' They entered. Inside there was nothing, a couple of disused ping-pong tables, some broken furniture. At the front there was a curtain.

'I thought you might like to watch,' the teacher said and pushed back the curtain, revealing a pane of glass, opening, miraculously, into light.

The woman came closer to the glass and leaned against it. Below, in the gym, a class was happening. She saw the fierce shape of a coach in the centre. Twenty young boys squatted on scattered blue mats, small heads, small bodies, in various states of stretching. She searched for the boy and found him, his body taut, ready to launch, and she held her breath.

You're Going to Forget Me

Before I Forget You

My sister called because she couldn't remember how to make small talk. She'd been having treatments with a doctor she'd encountered online. He specialised in torn minds. He helped women, specifically. It was a difficult process to discuss over the phone. When it first happened, she imagined the small talk words imprinted on the long, uncontrollable sausage-dog from our favourite childhood animation: off he went, walkabouts, his tail haughtily skimming the sky, the words she so desperately needed worn on his long body.

'That dog was so bold,' she said. 'Do you remember him?'

I did. The situation was that she could still discuss politics and art, if she wanted to discuss those things, which she usually didn't, but she couldn't say, 'Hey, how are you?' She was worried that this new development with small talk might lead people to dislike her in the workplace and other public settings; in her local coffee shop, for example. She would still, as a pregnant woman, like the pleasure of a small cake and an agreeable time. What was so wrong with that? 'Nothing wrong with that,' I said.

I switched the phone from my left ear to my right ear. I switched it back. Something about hotel rooms always made me feel like I was being detained, like a prisoner, before I would be released into another darker, more savage room. A room where I might have to defend myself.

On the other end of the line, my sister's voice – her neurosis so familiar, the same shape and texture as my own – inquired as to why people worried so relentlessly about being liked anyway? What was the big deal? It was, she said, only when people liked you too much that problems arose. Problems of possession. Problems of which coffee shops to attend after relationships fell apart. We were two fairly average women – lacking unique selling points, with figures that the magazines, in their general meanness, might accuse of being pear-shaped, hair that suggested frazzled, working minds – but even we had experienced the phenomenon of being liked.

Also she explained, for a brief time, after she lost the small talk, she didn't know what a fork was. Recently, she'd taken all the forks out of the kitchen drawer in the house she shared with her husband and closely examined them. She rested a fork on her growing belly. She managed to identify it as an eating tool. When her husband passed her a fork during the breakfast he insisted they shared every morning to strengthen their marital bond, she asked, 'What would you name this instrument?'

'Fork,' he answered.

In this way, my sister felt the matter was settled but she was worried a similar incident might occur with the knife, the lifelong boyfriend to the fork. Fondling the forks was just one of my sister's late night activities. The others, she said, weren't worth getting into. She was nearly seven months gone, a pregnancy at forty that the doctors described as 'geriatric.' We described it as miraculous. I listened, I listened, I half-listened. I was on a book tour and was, despite myself, despite the kind of person I encouraged myself to be by reading recommended deep literature, distracted by whatever hotel room I was sitting in – its flat design, creeping brownness and unfriendly furniture. Whenever my sister asked about the tour, or my work, which she found confusing and opaque and sort of disagreeable, like I'd started an argument I refused to finish, I simply said, 'I love it. I really love it. I believe in it.' Then we were silent for a long time.

'What's a person who talks constantly about what they like called?' my sister asked.

'A zealot.'

'Am I a zealot now that I can't do small talk?'

'I'm not sure. You could be.'

'Am I too chubby to be a zealot?'

'You're not chubby – you're pregnant. And, anyway, I think zealots can be chubby.'

'No I think their heightened states keep them pretty slim.' She paused. 'Do you know what I thought of the other day?'

'Isn't this small talk? Aren't you doing it right now?'

'I'm your sister,' she said. 'It's never small talk when we do it.'

*

My first book, the most successful, had been about two children, two sisters, who had an alien encounter. I wrote it when I was twenty-seven. People started to speak to me in completely new ways, as if I was now wired differently. Movie talk. I met movie men and their handshakes seemed to glide right through mine. There were sequels, a series that seemed not to have been written by me, but by a woman who resembled me, a woman with a steady stream of benign answers. It surprised me how little I wanted and, when I actually got something, I never knew what to do with it, except giggle, like a girl winning a school prize.

Time passed. I ate lunch with my agent. She blinked hard at me as if to say, 'Where is the new book?' She kept the rest of her body neutral. Blink, blink, blink. No book. Now the anniversary tour, where I sat, styled and tidy, in front of neat rows of children. In the lobbies, I was faceless, like a crude reproduction of myself. My phone was more real to me than the people I encountered. I was just an ear and, because I was lucky, another ear listened back.

My sister thought I was an interesting person because I presented as pleasant – I had a high, persuasive laugh and I wrote books for children – but I was deeply contrary. I was contrary in ways most people don't know how to be contrary. I was contrary in my bones. In a room with a desk and a bed and a chair, none of which were mine, I showered, watched the steam dissolve off my skin, and called my sister. The dial tone, two transformative beeps, and, on the other side, she was there.

'Do I have a temper problem?' I asked.

There had been some regrettable incidents in the past.

'Yes,' she admitted, 'but it's more like you're just stuck in bad traffic all the time. It's on the quieter end of the violent scale.'

My sister and I, from a young age, categorised our problems – facial, bodily, personality – marvelling at how easy it was to sort everything into a list. The certainty of a list. My main trouble, my sister declared, was that I always lived my life like I was immediately planning on leaving it.

'Buy a chair, buy a table, settle,' she insisted, her voice, for a second, distorted by the speaker. I looked around the hotel room, the dull impermanence of it. I thought of my own practically unfurnished apartment. People and the stuff they owned confused me – and it was confusion rather than any point I was trying to assert

about my own independence. Stuff tied them to the
world in a way I had no inclination for. I guess because
I never expected to be here too long.

'Was I always this way?' I asked.

She didn't answer. I repeated myself. She still didn't
answer.

'I don't know anymore,' she said, quietly.

*

When we were children, thirteen and nine, my sister and I
spent a summer in our local swimming pool. Our mother
was dead by then. Her illness happened mainly at home so
when I think of death now I can't conjure anything except
the stretch of brown linoleum leading to my parents'
bedroom. We heard her, through the transparent walls,
promise our father she wouldn't do it to him. But she did.

We never thought it would happen that way. You could
call us unprepared. You could call us hopeful. Startled
by our new single-parent freedom, my sister and I went
to the local swimming pool. The water was cloudy and
we charged into it in cheap, faded costumes. A memory
of my sister's triumphant face as she hit the filthy water.
She did lengths, her body slashing, appearing and disappearing, and I stood in the shallow end. Or she floated
on her back, with no trace of self-consciousness. Over
us, like a threat, hung a painted, shimmering sky. In the
changing room, as we slipped out of our clothes, my
sister spoke about the planet. After our mother passed
my sister had become obsessed with other planets. No,

not planets. One planet. That I never knew the name of, and nor could its dimensions be found on any of the star constellations charts I searched furiously.

*

Several of the people who came to the readings were grown-ups, or they passed as grown-ups. Late twenties, early thirties, and they glared at me from the back of the room, like I was still too young, or, suddenly, without permission, I was now too old. I was never sure which. Afterwards, they sloped off, maybe ashamed that a children's book still meant something to them. I had this gesture I did – it made me smirk – where I put my hands up as if to say, 'I don't have all the answers but, at the same time, I have most of the answers.' I crossed my legs. I sipped my water. I said some words about the imagination. That's just how it went. The problem was people asked boring questions and when they asked boring questions, I gave boring answers. But if someone had asked, even once, the right question, I would have told the truth. Mostly, it was young girls who enquired – the world kept spurting out young girls who looked at me in an awful, worshipping way – and what they always asked was, 'Do you have a sister in real life?'

'I do,' I would say.

Their follow-up questions were hard to predict.

'Is she tall?'

'She's slightly taller than me.'

'Is she your friend?'

'Yes,' I always said, 'she's a very good friend of mine.'

Finally, the microphone was switched off, the sound extinguished, and I went back to the hotel.

*

At one of the readings in a generic city, an older man, visibly nervous, the words sticking in his throat, stood up and asked if I thought there was a parallel world alongside this one, a world we knew nothing about? I said yes, I believe that to be true and he looked satisfied, like life had suddenly been solved. That night, when I returned to the hotel, anxious for reasons I couldn't identify, I rang a friend. He sounded relaxed, like he was lying down on the other end of this call. I wanted to say, 'Stand up, treat me with respect,' but it was far too late to start treating each other with respect.

'If you were,' I asked, 'to name a fork something other than "fork", what would you name it?'

He was silent. 'It's a fork. A fork is a fork.'

'I disagree. A fork is never just a fork.'

We had been in love once. It had been sloppy and hurtful. On the hotel television, static black lines, like determined swimmers, swept across the screen. I couldn't hold down furniture and I couldn't hold down people. It all just peeled away from me.

'If you want,' I said, 'you can hang up and I will just keep talking.'

He stayed on the line. Despite everything we had done to each other, we remained close.

*

My sister called me in the next hotel room – I tried not to acknowledge these rooms, the unending blankness of them, how they cruelly reflected my own life back at me – because she didn't know how to kiss anymore. She'd been sitting on the couch with her husband and he turned rapidly and put his face close to her face. It was alarming, seeing the bumpy forehead of her beloved looming over her. Then she knew, because of the expectant creases in his forehead, that there was a gesture required of her. She rested her nose against his nose and wiggled it. 'I opened my eyes wide,' she explained, 'as if to say, "I appreciate all of you."' That night, in bed, he rolled away from her.

'I think he wanted you to kiss him.'

'How do you kiss?' she asked.

'You just put your lips on someone else's lips and go from there.'

I remembered my sister, at thirteen, *forking* out a malevolent tongue at me. 'Tongues,' she announced, 'are for kissing.'

'Do you use tongue?' she whispered down the phone.

'Only if you really like the person. Do you really like your husband?'

She thought. 'Sometimes.'

*

I rang the doctor my sister had been seeing. I found his number online and, alone in hotel bars, I rang it. My

sister had reported a range of symptoms: shortness of
breath, dizziness, her memories spotting and blurring
like she was being reborn, her chest and stomach filling
with a substance that felt like water. I rang it hundreds of
times. I prepared what I would say. I would say, 'Hello,
I'm a woman who needs help,' although I had worked
hard my whole life to appear as if I never needed any
help. Nobody answered, not even a secretary. I could
see the phone ringing out in a dingy office by a car park,
or in a plush, velour room with a couch that forced you
to lie down and unfurl. A horror image of a sterilised
surgeon's clinic with strip lighting and stirrups invaded
my dreams nightly. I left messages. I did readings and,
somehow, even in my complete absence, the words
came out. I answered the questions that were put to me.

I remembered, ten years previously, the first lunch
I had with my agent, who told me, with a laughably
solemn expression, that not everybody was going to love
me. Here was my great, insurmountable problem, the
culmination of all the lists – not everybody was going to
love me. I didn't need everybody. I needed one person.
I rang that number.

*

My sister had only woken me in the middle of the night
once before in my life, but in another hotel room in
another city – exemplary in its tidiness, chocolates on
the pillow – she called, late, and asked me to smoke
down the phone to her.

'Have you forgotten how to smoke?'

'I'm eight months pregnant, idiot.' She paused. 'Please?'

I got up and pulled out a pack of cigarettes. I struck up a single match and rasped in the direction of the receiver. I pressed my smoky mouth to the screen, watched the weak blinking of the fire alarm.

'How's that?' I asked.

Somewhere, alone in the house she shared with her husband, she inhaled.

'That's nice,' she said. 'What time is it there?'

'Three.'

'So what do you tell people at these things when they ask how you got the idea?'

I rested my head on the bed frame, stubbed out the red light of the cigarette.

'I tell them I have a rich interior life.'

Water drizzled down on the bed. An alarm sounded. I closed my eyes and wished for the bed to become a blue swimming pool, into which I would lower myself, step by step, and sink.

*

After swimming, my sister and I always waited in the nearby tennis courts for our father. 'Here,' she said, 'is where they are going to land. A clear space so we can see the lights.'

I thought it was childish of her, at thirteen, to still play these games and her childishness, as it would in later years, embarrassed me. In the car on the way home, swimsuits soaking our clothes, our father sat silently.

As we drove – streets devoid of their gossipers, lamps angled skyward – the town seemed average. Sometimes, at night, it was capable of convincing you it was a normal place.

When we got home my sister washed my hair clean of chlorine in the kitchen sink, her fingers kneading my skull. Bent over, my shoulders cold against the ceramic, I felt sick as if a secret was going to be unearthed. At home, my sister handled things, but in her new school she was gaining a reputation. She had stopped finishing her sentences and her copybook consisted of blank lines where the words should have been. She vanished for hours on end. When my father asked her about it, she explained she was preparing for them so, when they came, she would be one of them.

One night, she took me from my bed and carried me to the swimming pool. They found us a day later. Two diligent swimmers arriving for 7 AM practice, discovered us in the pool, unconscious but fully clothed, early morning sunlight streaming in. When they heaved my sister's body out of the water, they realised she was bleeding. We found out later she had miscarried. Three months. I didn't need to be there to know that, upon this discovery, my father, like an animal, let out a low, intimate sound.

They kept us in hospital for two weeks, the scent of chlorine strong on our bodies. Every night, I held my right hand under the hot tap, watched the water flow off my palm. I wandered the hospital, its still, concrete hallways like a drained pool. For the hour I was allowed,

I visited my sister's bedside, pressed my warm palm to her forehead. She didn't smile or speak, but I wanted her to know I was there. Just once she sat up and said, 'Tell our mother you love her.'

'Our mother's gone.'

I thought maybe she had forgotten. There was bruising on her face and neck.

'Tell her anyway.'

*

The microphone was turned off, the sound extinguished, and I always went back to the hotel.

*

In the last hotel room, in the final city, my phone froze. I had been talking to my sister. I wanted to know how that doctor worked. I wanted to be in the treatment room. Was it gently psychological or did he apply shocks to her body? Was it electricity? What was the process? Was it painful?

My sister answered my questions abruptly.

'I wanted to have this baby,' she said.

'Was it painful?' I asked again, insistent.

The screen flashed bright then black.

I took the lift to the hotel bar. I had a drink. I wanted to use the phone but when I saw the barman, suited, assured, giving no indication that he was dying, or that anyone in his family was dying, or forgetting their lives, or losing something day by day, I was so angry that I was speechless. I thought of all the people who cared about him and how they would continue to care about him. So what I said instead was, 'I think this hotel is trash.'

He blew out his cheeks.

'It's not a personal thing,' I explained. 'I've decided all hotels are trash.'

'That's okay, ma'am.'

'I'm sorry. I've had a longish trip.'

'Did you enjoy your breakfast?'

'I did.'

'Good.'

There was a prolonged silence.

'May I use the phone?' I asked.

He placed a black, old-fashioned telephone on the counter and shuffled away. I made to call my sister but, in a resigned and desperate move I was familiar with, I called my friend. He answered. Ten years ago, meeting him, hearing his voice, felt like the start of my life. I wasn't a child anymore. Why couldn't I say it? What would it sound like?

'Would you forget me if you could?' I asked.

I hadn't moved on. I don't know how anybody moves on from anything.

'No,' he admitted. 'I wouldn't.'

*

When the barman called my room later that night and asked would I accept a call, I said no problem. I said a few words to him before my sister came on the line. I had told her the city, but I hadn't given her the name of the hotel, and I thought of the stream of numbers she must have punched to find me.

'You're worried I'm going to forget you.'

I didn't reply.

'No, not ever. Okay?'

'Okay,' I agreed.

She explained how she was forgetting our mother now. She remembered making our father's lunch, our wooden back door divided in two, how, when you stood outside, for a second, you were a half-person. She remembered holding me in her arms. But she couldn't see our mother, how she looked, or how her touch felt, or, towards the end of her life, what machines ran out of her body.

'Don't hang up tonight.'

I stayed on the line.

*

There is a moment when you get a call you don't want to receive, when you look at your phone as if it's to blame for the news it's about to impart, as if it's wholly responsible for this crime. Two separate films unspool in the dark. Then you answer it.

*

The news is never what you expect. My sister's husband told me what hospital she was in. Early labour. It was the same hospital we were kept in as children. I came straight from the airport. I pushed a button and doors slid open. There were doubtless many things happening in that hospital, as there are in hospitals all over the world, but I didn't notice any of them.

I walked those same hallways and everything I had done in my life up to that point felt absolutely worthless. I came to my sister's room. I sat on the edge of her bed and said, 'Hi.' She held her baby in her arms. She looked up, looked at me like she'd never seen me before in her life, like I was the faint trace of a person. 'Hey,' she said, very politely and slowly. 'Hey, how are you?'

Not the End Yet

The arranged place was not easy to find. Angela drove, her window rolled down. She knew if someone glanced inside her car, they would think: That woman's life has gone to shit, and she has been living, like a pig, in her car. She imagined the smug satisfaction such a person might derive from the scene: Things are hell for me but I don't live in my car! The world's dumb and uneven distribution of sadness was something she had no interest in. Let them have it, she thought. She knew she didn't live in her car. She lived in a house. Her car was in a state of disorder, yes, but then again so was her house. Except people couldn't see into her house. If they pressed themselves close to the glass she could simply say, 'Shoo, peepers!' and close the blinds. Her car didn't have blinds. Her car had an overflowing ashtray, a litter of coffee cups, clothes and bundles of coloured paper. Her house was in a row of other houses. She wasn't that invested in it. It was done when that was the theme – curbing, piping, structure. These days, it was taking her longer to get out of the car and into the house. But, she still did it. The upshot was: her life hadn't gone to shit.

The car park was deserted, except for a lone, hunched figure resting on the bonnet of a car, in communication with the cloudless night. This moonlit man was Angela's date. She rolled her tongue absently over her back teeth and watched through the windscreen as he cupped his hands and attempted to light a cigarette. Even as the wind ruined his efforts, he remained unruffled. This, to Angela, was a sign of huge integrity. She smoothed her skirt down over her hips and thighs. She checked her wide-eyed expression. She went slowly about her main-tenance. She was older now, forty-one. She would have been unaware of that herself, except people told her. The world practically crossed the street to tell a woman she had gotten older.

'What the fuck is that?' Angela's date said, gesturing to her car, as she rose gracefully from the driver's seat.

There was always a moment on Angela's dates, usually at the beginning, when she allowed herself to think: This guy's the whole package! As the night progressed, the realisation invariably arrived that this man was not a package at all. He was an envelope, an envelope with a bill in it, an envelope she, quite frankly, wanted to put in a drawer and forget all about.

She felt invaded by his judgement but refused to show it. 'It's a Honda,' she said, sweetly.

*

The restaurant was a basement really, with a damp smell of impending disaster and a neglected feeling. Angela and her suitors conducted all their encounters underground, in this place where the name changed frequently – letters disappearing, vowels skipping across the brightly lit sign – but the menu remained indifferent to external pressures. She chose this place because it had little or no phone signal. Otherwise, their fingers would be moving across their screens, sloppily swiping. When they swung the front door open, carrying in the heavy, co-mingled scent of perfume and aftershave, the staff stared at them. A teenage boy seated them with a reluctant sigh, as if exhaling was too much of an effort. Two further teenagers, stumbling at a furiously slow pace in true disbelief that anyone would demand service at this time, provided a tablecloth, cutlery, glasses. When Angela and her date (forty-five, salesman, no visible scars) gave their orders, the waiter nodded as if he might be willing to consider it.

Her date held up the menu in his paw hands, the familiar black marker scrawled across several of the selections. She ordered the salad, anticipating the single tomato rolling around her plate.

'So you go on many of these?' her companion asked, reddening. An entry to a dirty joke.

There was a deep silence and they let it labour between them for a moment.

'Yeah,' she replied. She had heard a lot of arguments against honesty in this particular arena, but she disregarded them. 'Make them feel special!' her oldest friend advised, but making people feel special required a lot of exertion and alcohol.

Although intimacy made her anxious and, often, physically sick, she had an absurd level of success in securing dates. In one careful photo taken at the wedding of a colleague, she sat beside a pristine table-cloth, her palms clasped like a choirgirl, her grin lopsided and benign. It was pleasant. You would have no problem being stuck in a tight dinner-space, island B&B or tiny house with this woman. You would barely know she was there. Other women engineered their profiles all wrong: too sexy, too obvious, their indecent mouths suggesting a closeness that had yet to be earned. She got a lot of attention for one particular set-up: hair loose, eyes alert. Soft. There was nothing to suggest she had made mistake after mistake after mistake.

'Is it much fun?' Her date (navy suit, tan shoes) fidgeted in his chair.

'Kind of.'

In truth, she had begun to approach these dates with the same level of clinical excitement as might accompany the scheduling of a dental appointment: the same dim sense of obligation, the same knowledge that a man was going to examine her and decide something was horribly awry. But she forced herself to enjoy it. It was the last good feeling, to look across a table and know someone else was terrified too.

'Right.' He nervously scanned the room.

They drank for something to do with their hands and mouths. Angela cursed her gin and tonic. It was impossible to look wise, and to project an air of disinterest in various earthly disasters, while using a straw.

'I said I was stopping after hitting ten,' he said. 'One zero. You know, with what's going on, some guys don't know how to stop. But I don't like this. I don't like superficial connections with people.'

'That's a shame,' Angela said. 'I love them.'

'Angela, I don't want to jump to any conclusions. I don't like conclusions, they are dangerous, but may I say something?'

'Go ahead.'

'On first read, you strike me as a cold person.'

She considered this for a moment, as it was not an unreasonable observation.

'I can be likeable if you get to know me,' she promised, silently wondering if this was true or one of those first-date lies she would have to catalogue and monitor. 'I just mean I never thought I would become one of those people who enjoys talking to strangers. I never thought my life would swerve off like that, but it has.'

'Tell me about your friends.'

'I have two,' Angela said, boastfully.

She was in possession of one old friend who offered helpful advice like, 'Have some self-respect!' Her old friend was full of bizarre ideas inherited from her time in business. She also had a friend in the supermarket. Where all her other friends had disappeared to was a mystery she had no interest in solving.

The silence became quite natural after a while. They ate their dinner to the beat of it.

He gleamed suddenly, as if he had made a discovery. 'What music do you like?'

'I like the classics,' Angela said.

'Oh yeah? Me too. Which ones?'

Angela threw open her arms and sang loudly but rushed, rendering the lyrics incomprehensible.

'I don't know that one.'

Her date's face was unmoving. And oddly small, she noted warily. It was an awfully tiny face.

'There's plenty more where that came from,' Angela promised. 'I have a lot of CDs in my car. I don't like the radio so much lately.'

'Nobody does,' he sighed. 'Who do you blame for it all?'

'It's not anybody's fault. That's what they say on the radio.'

'I have a few ideas,' he said, edgily. 'So what age are those kids you teach?'

'I'm not sure,' Angela smiled. 'They are short and move quickly in all sorts of directions.'

Out of Angela's class of twenty-six children, there were now only nine remaining. She sometimes passed absent students on the streets, riding or being pushed on scooters by their parents. The kids pretended not to know her. The remaining few spoke a language that was not from this planet, a language Angela couldn't understand. She distributed safety scissors and said, 'What's that?' loudly, to let them know she was on to them, curtail any uprising against her.

'It's good to have work you enjoy,' her date announced. Angela thought he looked restless, like he was gearing up to make some class of speech.

'Do you know what sort of man I used to be?'

'No idea.'

'I used to be the sort of man who always said, "I just need a break!" But now I'm making money for the first time in my life, selling dating equipment. What do you think of that, eh? You wait twenty years and – BOOM – all the money comes at once.'

'Money is no good when you're dead,' she intoned.

'I could have a younger girlfriend,' he said.

Angela could tell he was in the early stages of grief for someone he had never known.

'You are probably judging me for saying that.'

'Not at all.' She saluted him from across the table. 'It's a grand historical tradition.' She paused. 'Why do you do it anyway? It seems like a base job for a cosmopolitan individual, exploiting people's loneliness.'

'Cash,' he said. He stared past her, to the front door. 'I have gambling debts.' He hesitated. 'It's probably something to do with my father as well.'

'The excuse that never dies,' Angela said. 'Something something my father. I swear when the world does end, there's just going to be one man meandering around the scorched earth saying again and again: "I had a bad relationship with my father."'

'Are you a feminist?' he asked abruptly, as if she might be surprised he knew the word.

'At this stage in my life, I can take it or leave it,' she replied. She lit a cigarette and watched the smoke swirl up towards the splintered ceiling. Witnessing her defiance, one of the teenagers glared at her through the long bar mirror. She was waiting for her date to mention an ex-wife. She wanted to run into the past and scatter these women like birds.

'Were you married?' she asked.

'I was,' he said and looked at her in a practised, sheepish way.

Angela shifted in her seat, preparing for her own declaration. She gazed off into space. 'There's a time in a woman's life when everyone she is sleeping with is married, then there's the extended period of time when she may be married herself, then suddenly everyone she is sleeping with is divorced.'

'That's an interesting theory.'

'It's just an old saying of my mother's,' she shrugged.

'Well,' he said, 'no one gets off lightly – my dog is dead, my bicycle is destroyed, my life is a bit messed up, to put it mildly. But that's marriage, isn't it?' He nodded as if in sincere agreement with himself. 'You?'

'I got the car in the divorce.'

He smirked. 'Kids?'

She made a zero figure with her thumb and wedding-ring finger. 'So,' she asked and dipped her finger into the surface of her drink, 'have you been doing anything?'

'This,' he said, pointing back and forth between them. 'A lot of this, interacting with new people.'

'Same.'

There had been a series of bad dates recently. There was the man with a face of deep crevices and dents who, up close, looked rather like the moon. There was another who rested his slithery hand on hers while trying to sell her life insurance. No matter how many times Angela thought *That's not happening again*, it happened. It happened and it happened. It was all over quickly, but it happened. Dating was not the worst of it though.

Angela cleared her throat. 'I did something else.' She closed her eyes, as if preparing for confession. 'I stole a cat.'

'Excuse me?'

'There has been a cat hanging around the school grounds and, today, I bundled it up under my coat and took it home. It did not belong to me in any way,' she grinned, 'but now it does.'

'Why?'

'Firstly, it had a great look. If sunglasses were an option for this cat, he would have been wearing them. I have always been weak for that sort of coolness. Also my principal told me if it was still there by the end of the week, he was going to cook and eat it.'

'Jesus Christ, that's disgusting.'

'It is,' Angela said, 'but that's him all over. It's his nature. He'd do it because the world's ending and he can. I would use the word "lunatic" to describe him. First day, he separated all us female teachers into two groups. He didn't say it but I could see his mind working: the women he wanted to sleep with, and the women he considered good teachers.'

'Which group were you in?'

'Neither.' Angela gestured for a second drink. 'But you should have heard the arguments in the staff room: he wants to lick me up and down, he wants to mentor me. I eat lunch in my car a lot.' Angela was suddenly passionate. 'You know, there is a lot I will tolerate in this life, and a lot I have tolerated, but the cooking and eating of a cat to prove you're a tough guy is not a pursuit I will entertain.' She looked down at her napkin, surprised by her sudden outburst.

'Have you named the cat?'

'Screechy.'

'That's a gorgeous name.' Her date looked at her with warmth. 'Angela, I got you wrong. I apologise. You're a kind and considerate woman.'

'Stop,' she said stiffly. 'I have some interesting qualities too.'

'I never thought I would meet a nice woman, let alone another animal-lover.' He paused. 'I don't want to paint her in a negative light, but my ex-wife murdered my dog.'

'I guessed that.'

'Imagine that bathroom in there,' he pointed to the restaurant bathroom, 'normal bathroom, tiles, bit of mould, nothing spectacular.'

'I can see it.'

'Now picture it with blood everywhere. That was how it was. A disappointing sight.'

'I'm sorry,' Angela said.

'What was up with your ex?'

'He was non-violent. He didn't murder anything, as far as I know. All in all, an agreeable man.' She paused. 'Do you like clever people?'

'Not really.'

'You would have liked him then. He wasn't clever at all. It wasn't a big deal like people make it out to be.' She looked at him. 'Not that he was an imbecile either.'

'What is it all for, Angela? Sometimes, when I am selling them the damn equipment I want to say, "Don't bother," but I can't because of the money and the commission.'

'I have an old friend who thinks it's for companionship. Someone to hold your hand at the end, that sort of thing.'

'I don't like the sound of your friend much,' he said.

'Yeah,' she agreed. 'She's not great. It's terrible when you get old enough to dislike your old friends.'

She glanced down; her salad was gone. She had no recollection of putting that fork in her mouth. Her body was always making decisions independent of her.

'Angela, would I be correct in saying we have a deep and profound connection at this present moment in time?'

'You wouldn't be too far off.' She pondered. 'Would you like to sit in my car with me for a while?'

When they stood to leave, the teenagers gathered in a circle and unenthusiastically waved them off. As they settled the bill, the man interlaced his fingers with Angela's. One of the serving boys made a discreet retching face at this display of middle-aged affection. In the car park, her date said, 'Look, the stars are low,' – and they were.

In her car, they sat in silence. Her date rested his feet impolitely on the dashboard. He looked like a monarch, surveying his kingdom.

'You know that number I gave you?' Angela asked.

'Your telephone number?'

'Yeah. If you are going to use that number the best time is between 5 PM and 8 PM because that is after school and before night.'

'What do you do at night?'

'I go to the supermarket,' Angela said simply.

'Is it … nice in the supermarket?'

'It's a good time,' Angela said. 'I have a friend there.'

They both stared out the windscreen.

'Angela, I want to take you home. But before I take you home, can I tell you something?'

'Sure.'

'Men are after me. Threatening men I encountered during my gambling period.' He slouched dramatically in his seat. 'I would like to spend the night with you but I don't want to put you in a bad situation. In truth, I'm being blackmailed and I'm being followed.' He let out a long, weary sigh and ran his hands over his face, as if the blackmailing would be okay if it weren't accompanied by the following, and the following would be fine if it weren't accompanied by the blackmailing.

'I have never dated a man who was being blackmailed before.' She paused. 'We can take my car if you think that will throw them off?'

He glanced around Angela's car. 'We will take mine, I think.'

He took Angela home and banged her like he was partaking in a burglary – ransacking the house for something he would never find. Angela was confused, but alive. This could be it: the last neck they clawed at, the last post-coital conversation, the last beautiful excuses they ever made.

The morning came while she was still feigning sleep. Before the sun even lit across her body, he was back on his dating equipment. The man was determined he was not departing from this planet with Angela's cursed face as his final conquest. Fair enough, Angela thought. These were testing times and she was recently big on forgiveness. It was being pushed heavily on the radio. Sometimes, she left these situations feeling something near happiness. Leaving was such a non-event. You turned a doorknob either to the left, or to the right. Leaving was the same everywhere.

That night, she took her usual trip to the 24-hour supermarket. She strolled around, swinging her wire shopping basket, the empty aisles opening out in front of her. She used to come here with her ex-husband in the sunny days of their courtship. They placed healthful items in baskets, their bodies slyly touching as they strolled. Now, the cashier girls wandered around, indifferent, as if this supermarket wasn't once the site of a Great Romance. She said, 'Oh, girls, I just want you all to be so happy,' and tried not to cry. That particular Saturday, she watched the artificial rain falling on the vacant spaces where the greens used to be displayed. She admired the labels: their verve, their refusal to stop selling themselves even in the direst circumstances. She put in orders for exotic fruits, fruits that would never pass her lips, and the girls wrote them dutifully down, avoiding her gaze.

*

The restaurant was a basement, really, with a damp smell of impending disaster and a neglected feeling. Inside, the waiters kept their jackets on over their uniforms, expecting to be called away at a moment's notice. There were only two waiters left from the previous staff of six. They hugged the menus to their chests, as if in possession of ancient secrets. The windows were fully covered. Angela and her date (forty-seven, artist, no visible scars) had just been to the theatre. Theatre wasn't something she normally did – and the imminent end of the world wasn't the time for trying new things – but, regardless, they attended the theatre. They had sat on a long, hard bench, their knees touching, then not-touching, then occasionally touching again at moments of dramatic seriousness. The touching was electrifying to Angela. It gave her a powerful rush to the head. The play didn't do much for her at all, at all.

'I'm not sure,' Angela said. 'I didn't get it.'

'What didn't you get?'

'All of it, it has to be said.'

There was one other couple in the restaurant, young and disturbingly beautiful, their smiles wide and postures primed as if in constant pose for a photo. They glanced over as Angela and her date began to raise their voices.

'That's a very ignorant point of view,' her date said.

'It is, I agree. My own ignorance is my business though, and I don't feel the need to explain or justify it to anyone.'

'Didn't you like the way their naked bodies symbolised their vulnerability in the face of the end of the world?'

'No.'

'And the dancing as the earth opened up below them? Their bravery? Their joy? Didn't you like that?'

'No.'

'Angela, I don't want to put pressure on you but if you didn't enjoy and appreciate that play, you're not going to understand me, fundamentally, as a human being.'

'That's okay,' she said.

The surlier of the two waiters approached them and set down their near-empty plates. Angela's date suddenly began grabbing at the dinner items as if to speed up the process.

'Don't do that,' she instructed, 'that's his paid employment.'

The artist whipped out his napkin and produced a pen. 'Angela, what is your ex-husband's address?'

'Why?'

'I would like to send him a card in the post, just a small token, to show him his hard work didn't go unnoticed. I believe people should be thanked for the duties they have performed in this life and you must have been a handful.'

'I was,' she agreed. 'I was like a long day's labour in the sun. You would emerge disorientated and physically exhausted, but stronger for it.'

His hand hovered excitedly over the napkin, as if planning exactly what to write inside his card.

'I'm sorry I don't know his address. I know he lives alone in an apartment but I couldn't tell you which one. It's a block of apartments with other men who live alone.'

Her date leaned backwards and performed a waving motion with his hand, as if trying to communicate with Angela's ex-husband from a distance. 'What age are those kids you teach?' he said, through a mouthful of lettuce.

'I don't know,' she said. 'They are short and move quickly in all sorts of directions.'

Her date (wide-legged jeans, shirt from a disco decade) looked desperately at the young couple across the restaurant as if wishing to signal his immense distress.

'You know what I didn't like about that play?' Angela didn't know how to let things go.

'What?'

'The way it was about the end of the world. Doomsday stuff. That felt obvious to me.'

'But that's what is happening right now. That's life,' he said, and the way he emphasised life made Angela want to throw her knife and fork at him. She would have done it too, had she not been nervous of the ire of the waiters.

'Yes, exactly. It's happening. I don't need to see it on stage.'

'I don't think you like art, Angela.'

'Maybe I don't,' she said, thoughtfully. 'I think I'm too anxious to spend long periods of time looking at things trying to figure out what they are.'

'You know what else I think you don't like?'

'What?'

'Nudity. Oh God, you're just like my ex-wife. A prude – exactly like her. I bet if I got naked right now you would have a problem with that.'

The young angel-boy leapt out of his seat and dashed to his girlfriend's side. He placed his hands over her unbelieving eyes as Angela's date began unbuttoning his shirt. The waiters let him get to the third button before they intervened. There was a brief bout of wrestling before Angela's date, out of breath, fully-dressed and furious, sat back down.

Angela exhaled a long, delightful plume of smoke.

'I'm having such a nice time,' she said. 'After dessert, would you like to sit in my car with me for a while?'

In Angela's car, they listened to the radio. Two men with the wild intensity of actors were shouting about disease and rising sea levels. One of the radio presenters said he had been having bad dreams, the other said he hadn't been sleeping at all. Finally, the more innovative of the two screamed, a thin piercing sound that rattled Angela's car and further reduced its life span.

'These people shouldn't be allowed on the radio,' she said.

As the presenters listed out the odds for the human race – which were not favourable from what Angela could tell – her date made to kiss her. She turned away at the final moment.

'Would you like to see a picture of my cat?' Angela inquired, as a token of peace.

'No,' he replied, sulkily.

Without a further word, he stormed out of the car, slamming the door behind him. She watched through the windscreen as he ruffled his hair and popped the top button of his shirt, creating a bedroom look. When the young couple emerged from the restaurant, he stopped the boy and offered a high-five, as if to celebrate his incredible sexual success in the car.

Angela thought: I'm never coming to this restaurant again. Never again.

*

The restaurant was a basement, really, with a damp smell of impending disaster and a neglected feeling. The waiters hung around in stained vests, helping themselves to drinks from the bar. Music Angela had never heard before was being piped through the speakers: loud, explicit and full of pushy directions. 'Get low,' this music advised and the waiters obliged by limboing underneath the entrance to the wooden bar. Each limbo was followed by a supportive whoop from a fellow waiter.

When Angela and her date (fifty, fruit and vegetable man, one faded scar running across his cheek) entered the restaurant, one of the waiters embraced Angela like she was a cousin who reminded him of carefree memories from his childhood. Plaster and dust from the ceiling littered the abandoned tables. A sign, in sloppy teenage handwriting, read: 'Only Dessert Available.' At a table nearby, sat a shabby-seeming couple and their young daughter, sharing a single slice of chocolate cake.

'This place is usually wall-to-wall sophisticated people,' Angela told the man.

The waiters, out of unquestioned routine, threw them two dinner menus. Angela shouted across to them, 'This fellow isn't my date.'

Her date raised his head in alarm.

'He's more of a guest,' she explained. 'He's employed in the local supermarket.'

The waiters ignored her.

'It's not always easy to recognise people out of their work uniforms,' she said. 'You look nice.'

'How is the school coping?' The fruit and vegetable man shredded his napkin nervously. He glanced at the waiters as if to find an answer to the apocalypse in their unruly behaviour.

'The staff room,' Angela shook out a cigarette, 'is pure farce at this point.'

'What do you get up to in there? I've always wanted to know.'

'Talking. Rage.'

A few days previously, the end date named, one of the older teachers had taken to wearing a veil – a wispy, fluttery piece of fabric that obscured her hunted face – as a gesture of mourning. Soon, she had amassed followers, a group of impressionable teachers who moved in a slow pack wearing makeshift veils fashioned from household materials. 'We just listen to the radio, eat sandwiches,' Angela said. 'Think regretfully about our lives.'

'Great!' he said. 'I just want to inform you this is a date.'

'Is it?'

'It is. I have seen you around the supermarket and I always thought I would like to show that woman some-where nicer than a supermarket – like a museum. We don't have much time left but would you like to go to a museum?'

'I like the supermarket,' Angela said. She pictured the hideous fluorescent lighting, the disappointing stock, the scowling staff in their polyester fleeces. 'I think some of the happiest moments of my life have taken place in that supermarket.'

'You would look good walking around a museum, I think.'

She ignored the compliment. 'So,' she said, eyeing up the rotating desserts, 'have you been doing anything?'

'I prayed.' He perked up at the memory of his brief interaction with God. 'I also lit a candle in a church.'

'Wow,' Angela said, in genuine awe. 'I stole a cat. I didn't necessarily steal it. I just looked at it and it came with me. I don't consider myself a sexually aggressive person but it's possible I seduced that cat.'

The little girl at the next table over vomited chunks of chocolate cake across the tablecloth. She carefully wiped her mouth, as if in preparation for a second round.

'I'm sorry,' the mother announced to the waiters. 'She's just nervous, I'm sorry.'

The waiters nodded in unison but made no move to clean up.

'That's one of mine,' Angela said. 'She's been doing that a lot lately.'

'She's in your class?'

'Yeah.'

'Say hello.'

'I'd rather not,' she said. 'They don't like me so much, the children.'

'I imagine you are a good teacher, Angela.'

'Oh, I do my best,' Angela said. This was true, maybe once. She had kept a close eye. There were still accidents on her watch, of course. A scratched elbow, a stone that had to be wrenched free. The children would rest their bodies on her lap. They would rise up then, recovered and forgetful. At the end of the day, no matter what she did, they left with whoever came to collect them. Children could be as breezy and carefree as adults.

'Today, I had to write "China: Wiped Out" on the board. Doubly underlined.' She managed a weak half-smile.

'How did that go?'

'Lots of questions: "Why are we still here, teacher?" "How do you spell that, teacher?" That sort of thing. The afternoon dragged right on.'

'It's hard to know how to fill the time,' he agreed.

At the other table, the little girl was crying, clutching her stomach with one hand and attempting to eat the remains of the cake with the other. Her parents observed her, their hands flat on the table in front of them, skilfully avoiding the vomit.

The fruit and vegetable man watched the family for a moment before turning back towards Angela. 'Have you been in contact with anyone?' he asked.

'No.'

'Me neither. My ex-wife, she *would* just disappear. Even when she was there, she wasn't there.'

'My ex-husband lives alone. He lives in a block of apartments with other men who live alone.'

'Kids?'

She made a zero figure with her thumb and wedding-ring finger. 'Well one actually,' she admitted, 'but he died. Do you mind me saying that? Not really died,' she corrected herself, 'got away from us early.'

'Did you try again?'

'No.'

'Why not?'

'He wanted to. I was scared.'

'Scared of death? That's natural.'

'No,' Angela said, 'scared of everything else.'

'My ex-wife used to say I wasn't ambitious,' the man explained. 'Afraid to progress from the fruit and veg section, but I explained it was just because I really liked fruit and vegetables and I wasn't going to fight it any longer.'

She laughed. 'Do you know what I find amazing about this world? What I will miss? How you can wander around looking like other people, but not really be like other people at all.'

'In what way are you not like other people?' The fruit and vegetable man gestured determinedly at the dessert tray.

'The child didn't like his surroundings, that's what the doctor told me,' she said. 'Like even a foetus couldn't bear to spend time with me.'

'What did you do?'

'I screamed, "Look around, moron, who does like their surroundings? I wouldn't rush myself to get here either."'

One of the waiters, sweating heavily, chose this moment to slop the unappetising carrot cake in front of them. They took a fork each.

'Do you think that's small? Being a woman who screams in a doctor's office?'

'Not at all.'

'It's not something I had planned for myself.'

They both took huge mouthfuls of cake, crumbs spilling indelicately on the table.

'So, what music do you like?' Angela asked.

'I like the classics. The oldies.'

Angela threw her arms open and sang loudly.

'That's one of my all-time favourites. I love that one,' he said. 'So tell me how you met your ex-husband?'

The family stood up and, without discussion, the girl bundled up in her father's arms, left the restaurant. Their exit brought in a blast of cold air and a quick glimpse of the outside space. The car park, the street lamps, the fluorescent restaurant sign – soon they would be gone. And then the restaurant itself, and whatever followed after that and after that. It would all go.

A wail silenced the restaurant. A teenage body lay unconscious on the floor. The waiters gathered cautiously around their brother, as if shocked by consequences at a time when there weren't supposed to be any consequences.

Angela stared directly at her guest. 'I had wanted him to stay, you know,' she said. 'But I didn't know how to say that. That one word seemed like a big word. I couldn't find a way into it. And I was afraid of what might happen if I even tried.'

He sat up straight, smiled wanly in her direction.

'Don't look too delighted,' she said. 'I took him to the cleaners in the divorce. Got the car and everything.'

Her guest put down his fork, struggling for the words like a man who has spent a long time without company, living alone in an apartment complex with other men who live alone.

*

The car dealership was on the outskirts of town. She expected to find it abandoned, but no – through the windscreen she watched the man behind the counter swinging gloomily on his swing chair. He had the look of someone who might have debated wearing a cowboy hat to hawk his goods, but was persuaded out of it by a sensible person aware of cowboy hats and what they could do to a man's reputation. The tinkling bell announced the arrival of Angela – a tall woman, a handsome woman, a woman with a cat peeking out from underneath her coat – and the counter-man's disappointment was plain. He would not be able to tell Angela what he told men: that cars brought a certain type of life, a certain type of woman, a certain type of insane luck. Angela just wanted to sit in a car for one last time, enjoy the new car smell, and not feel fear or disappointment. In the window of the car dealership there was a convertible rotating sleekly in defiance of all the outside decay.

'How much is that?' she asked.

The man, his belly swinging bountifully, spread his arms out wide, a move Angela suspected he had been practising in new and used cars during his downtime. It was a clear and direct arm-spread: it said, 'Angela, you are going to love it. You probably dismissed the sports car experience at some stage, we all have. You probably have thought – that's not for me. But you're going to adore it. Every last bitter second.'

Angela fitted snugly in the leathered front seat and Screechy mewed appreciatively. It was a car that could make a singular impression. Yes, Angela thought, as she exited the car dealership, that's smooth. On the radio, the announcer said we should be frightened, very frightened, and Angela looked at the sky: a fantastic scene of pinks and reds.

Acknowledgements

Many thanks to the editors of the publications in which early versions of these stories first appeared – *The Stinging Fly*, the *Dublin Review, Winter Papers* and the *White Review*.

A debt of gratitude is owed to the Arts Council for their continued support. A special thanks to Annaghmakerrig and the Irish Cultural Centre in Paris, where two of these stories were written.

A huge thanks to Alexis Kirschbaum, Liese Mayer and the team at Bloomsbury.

To Colin Barrett and Tom Morris for their invaluable feedback and encouragement.

To the Wylie Agency, particularly Tracy Bohan, a kind and smart presence throughout the entire publication process.

To Declan Meade for his endless patience and support.

Finally to my family, my parents and sister, for everything.

Note on the Author

Nicole Flattery is the author of the story collection *Show Them a Good Time* and the novel *Nothing Special*. She is the winner of the An Post Irish Book Award, the Kate O'Brien Award, the London Magazine Prize for Debut Fiction and the White Review Short Story Prize. Her work has appeared in the *Stinging Fly*, the *Guardian*, the *White Review* and the *London Review of Books*. She lives in Dublin, Ireland.